ParaNorman

A Novel

by Elizabeth Cody Kimmel

Based on the animated feature screenplay by

Chris Butler

Illustrated by Ross Stewart

Little, Brown and Company
New York Boston

Also by Elizabeth Cody Kimmel:

Suddenly Supernatural: School Spirit
Suddenly Supernatural: Scaredy Kat
Suddenly Supernatural: Unhappy Medium
Suddenly Supernatural: Crossing Over

—————

LAIKA

Little, Brown and Company

Hachette Book Group
237 Park Avenue, New York, NY 10017
Visit our website at www.lb-kids.com

Little, Brown and Company is a division of Hachette Book Group, Inc. The Little, Brown name and logo are trademarks of Hachette Book Group, Inc.

The publisher is not responsible for websites (or their content) that are not owned by the publisher.

First Paperback Edition: August 2013
First published in hardcover in June 2012 by Little, Brown and Company

ISBN 978-0-316-20986-1 (hc) / ISBN 978-0-316-20987-8 (pb)

10 9 8 7 6 5 4 3 2 1

RRD-C

Printed in the United States of America

For Emma Cody Kimmel

Then the Blithe Hollow Witch placed a
dreadful curse upon the judge and jury.

Prologue

"You have been arraigned for the detestable arts of witch-craft and sorcery. You have feloniously and maliciously performed evil works against your fellow townspeople, witnessed by these good citizens who have gathered here to render their testimony. Have you anything to say to the court at this time? Are you prepared to admit your evil works and repent?

"Very well, then, good people of Blithe Hollow. By thy witness, she will neither confess nor repent. Keep your hearts clear in the knowledge that she has denied this final opportunity to burn this sin from her soul by confession. You have, by the jury of these six peers empowered by our sovereign, King James, been found guilty of all the grievous crimes of which you are accused. The punishment is death. . . . No, witch, it is too late for you to speak. Silence, witch! Good jurors and townspeople, be not fear-ful. There is no curse. There is no curse!"

"Let's see. According to this, you are a common toad. Latin genus name *Bufo bufo*."

Chapter One

On the day Norman Babcock was born, *strange things* happened. Norman heard some of the birthday stories right from his own mother—how all the lights in the maternity ward blew their fuses at the very moment the doctor announced, "It's a boy!" How the dogs across town set up a strange chorus of howling right around that same time. How two guys coming off their shift at Witchy Weiner saw a rainbow in the sky—which might not sound that weird but really was when you added in the details that it was one in the morning and that the rainbow was shaped like a huge question mark.... Well, that's what they said. (It could have just been indigestion, though.)

So when a toad floating in a jar of bad-smelling stuff to keep it perfectly preserved began waving at Norman right there in the middle of Mr. Feynman's seventh-grade bio class, Norman was not surprised. He was not surprised at all. His ability to communicate with the dead wasn't limited to humans—animal ghosts had a lot to say, too, in their own way.

Norman waved back at the toad, who seemed pleased to be acknowledged. It almost looked as if it was giving Norman a gummy smile, but the amphibian caught sight of someone at the back of the classroom. Its face turned pale, as much as that was possible for a dead toad.

Norman knew who sat at the back of the classroom, near the spider terrarium and the old hamster ball (abandoned since the sudden disappearance of the hamster last Tuesday) and the pink plastic pig that had been sliced down the middle to give the curious a good look at the inner workings of the porcine digestive system.

"Yeah, that's Alvin," Norman told the toad. "He likes to hit stuff. Think of him as our token Cro-Magnon boy. No disrespect to cavemen, though."

The toad blinked its bulbous eyes and made no expression, as if to suggest its utter acceptance of this description.

"Sad but true," Norman said, running one hand

through his shock of dark brown hair, which stood straight up on his head like it was trying to escape.

The toad made a small croak, as if to whisper a secret, so Norman leaned in really close, his nose almost pressed up against the glass.

The toad eyeballed Norman, then looked down at itself. Then it flicked its tongue out to point to the classroom door.

"You want to go to a different room?" Norman asked.

The toad shook its head.

There was a sudden burst of laughter from the back of the room.

"No way!" came a voice that sounded like the start of a bad sound track to an even-worse production of *The Bullies of Blithe Hollow.* "Dudes, for real—Norman is *talking* to his frog! Alvin says that ain't normal!"

Norman sighed, bracing himself for a classic Alvin Attack. Mr. Feynman had a reputation for disappearing into the faculty bathroom with his newspaper when his students were supposed to be recording "scientific observations," so Norman knew there would be no help from that quarter.

"What's the frog sayin' to you, Norman?" Alvin sang. "Does he want to be best frog friends forever?"

The toad sighed, too, and gave Norman an irritated look, gesturing at a label, yellowed with age and partly peeling off its jar.

"You're not a frog; you're a toad," Norman said. "Yeah, you must get so tired of people making that mistake. Let's see. According to this, you are a common toad. Latin genus name *Bufo bufo*."

The little creature nodded with evident pride.

Alvin erupted in one of his patented Alvin Hyena Laughs, one that Norman was secretly sure involved at least a small amount of pants-wetting.

"Dudes, did you hear that? Norman named his new friend Boofo Boofo! I think this is it—I think Normie has finally gone Boofo Boofo himself! Call the guys in the white jackets!"

"*Bufo bufo*, the common toad, of the family of true toads, Bufonidae," stated a high, prim voice coming from just behind Norman.

The toad's expression brightened, and it tried to float to the right a little so it could get a glimpse of who had just spoken.

"That's Salma," Norman said, sitting with his chin

in his hands, waiting for something to land on Alvin—a lightning bolt or a band of crazed winged monkeys—anything that might unexpectedly silence him. "She's a brain."

"Brown or green in color, they are toothless and sometimes warty in appearance," Salma continued.

The toad looked a little embarrassed by that and ran one webby foot over its head, as if checking for new warts.

"Is there something wrong with your *Bufo bufo*?" Salma asked Norman.

"I don't know," Norman said. "I mean, it's already dead and in a jar—what else can happen to it?"

The toad pushed both webbed feet up as if it were trying to lift the lid off the jar.

"You want out of the jar," Norman said, and the toad nodded.

"But you're, um…dead and all that," Norman pointed out, as kindly as he could.

The toad tucked its feet under its chin and closed its eyes.

"Oh. Now I understand," Norman said. And he did. Perfectly.

"What?" Salma asked.

"It wants a proper grave," Norman said. The toad opened its eyes and croaked enthusiastically.

"I get it," Norman told it. "You just want to rest in peace."

Norman felt something poke his arm. He glanced in the direction of the plump finger attached to the meaty arm coming out of the roundness that was Neil Downe.

"Norman, come on, man," Neil whispered. "Take it down a notch. Stop talking to your bio project. You're giving Alvin tons of ammo here—he's going to be giving you grief for days!"

That was pretty rich, Neil Downe telling anybody to take it down a notch. Neil was chubbier than any other kid in school, his hair was redder and frizzier, and his voice was squeakier. Also, he had a lunch box with a kitten on it. And that's just for starters. Neil always acted all friendly to Norman, but he just didn't get it—Norman didn't need friends.

"Whatever," Norman said, turning away in his seat and repositioning the toad's jar so Neil couldn't see it. "Give me a minute or two to come up with a plan," he told the toad.

"Oh wait.... Norman only plays with dead things," came Alvin's bleating voice. "He must be talking to a ghost frog! Hah, that's it! Norman's a ghost-frog whisperer!"

Alvin cracked himself up bad with that last remark. He was making this gross wheezing noise as he laughed, and his mouth sounded kind of full, like he had forgotten to swallow. He'd be drooling soon.

"Do you mind?" Salma said to Alvin sharply. "Some of us are trying to create a Venn diagram for our organisms by taxonomic classification."

"Like, duh!" Alvin spluttered. "Salma's origami is the *classiest!*"

The toad scowled. Norman looked at its warty head and got an idea. He turned around and looked at Alvin.

"That thing on your thumb is a wart, and it's never going to go away, no matter what you do," Norman stated.

Alvin's mouth dropped open midcackle. He extended his thumb in front of his face and squinted at it, his eyebrows furrowed in concentration. He looked like a mountain gorilla trying to figure out what a Game Boy was—except not as intelligent.

Norman sighed with relief, glad he had distracted Alvin, and then turned back to the jar. The toad's ghost was floating slightly above its body, which bobbed up and down in the bad-smelling stuff. Norman could see a faint image of his own face reflected in the glass, his deep blue eyes looking weirdly disembodied.

Neil Downe was right about one thing. Norman had given Alvin plenty of bullying ammo by talking to a dead toad in bio class. Stealing the toad would probably make things much worse. For the next couple of days, maybe even the next week, gym class and lunch were going to be brutal.

But this was what Norman did. He'd been seeing and hearing ghosts for as long as he could remember, and he'd finally started talking back to them about a year ago, just around the time his grandmother died. The dead toad wasn't the only spirit who needed Norman to do him a favor. Blithe Hollow was utterly teeming with phantom people and animals competing for Norman's attention. He talked to every single one of them wherever they found him—walking home from school, on the playground, over at Witchy Weiner. If that made him an outcast, well, whatever. Norman had never really been too keen on being an *in*cast in the first place. As far as he could tell, most living people were vastly overrated.

"Okay," Norman told the toad. "I think I have a plan to get you out of here."

As the toad swam in a circle in delight, Mr. Feynman returned to the classroom. At about the same time, the missing hamster shot out from behind a dusty display labeled THE JOY OF INVERTEBRATES and began careening from one end of the room to the other. Someone yelled, "It's a mouse!" And someone else shouted, "It's a rat!" And Neil Downe shrieked, "It has rabies!" And that was about the time Alvin began screaming like a girl, Salma put her hands over her ears, and the fire alarm went off.

In all the commotion, nobody noticed Norman putting his books in his bag, tucking the toad's jar under one arm, and walking out of the classroom. He might get a pink slip from the hall monitor or a tardy mark from the cafeteria monitor, but Norman didn't care. He slipped out the side door near the playground and headed to a swampy little spot just beyond the swing set. He'd worry about Alvin and pink slips later.

Right now, he had some eternal rest to take care of.

"There's a library book in my office, and I'm just not going to be able to get any eternal rest until someone takes it back."

Chapter Two

Grandma Babcock's funeral had been disturbing for a number of reasons.

First, obviously, was the fact that it *was* a funeral. Grandma Babcock had been super old, and she'd died very peacefully sitting on the couch watching *As the Doctors' Day Turns*, which was her favorite program. But Norman missed Grandma, and judging by the eye-makeup smudges and the lack of rude comments, so did his sister, Courtney. Norman's parents had both asked him about twenty times to not do anything "not normal" during the funeral. His dad was also very tense about some crazy old uncle they were afraid would show up and make a scene. If there was anything Perry Babcock hated in the world, it was having the wrong kind of attention drawn to his family. Which, unfortunately, seemed to happen a lot when Norman was around.

Norman didn't plan to do anything but stand by the refreshment table and avoid people. Courtney kept going into the ladies' room and coming out with her makeup even more smudged, so Norman decided to leave her alone, too. Anyway, he preferred to enjoy his own memories of his grandmother, rather than being asked the same old questions by thirty different people. It wasn't like he would never see her again. Norman had been seeing ghosts since he could remember, and chances were, Grandma Babcock would show up sooner or later. But nobody else would be able to see her, and that was bound to cause complications. The dead always did.

When you can see dead people, you are instantly very popular—but only among dead people. So Norman hadn't been in the funeral home for more than ten minutes when a group of noisy ghosts gathered around him.

"Listen, it's only a one-sentence message: 'The mayonnaise in the fridge has gone bad.' Can you just tell her that, please?"

The gauzy, glowing image of a bookish old guy in a striped sweater-vest and thick glasses bobbed anxiously in front of him. Little luminous spirit orbs wafted gently around his head. Norman didn't respond, so the guy just repeated his question louder.

"Well, I could try," Norman said, trying not to look like he was talking. He'd never actually talked back to a ghost before, at least not in front of anybody.

"Wait, my message is only one sentence, too," said a large, blue-haired woman holding an enormous purse. "It's this: 'The cats do not like to be bathed.' Can you tell him that? 'The cats do not like to be bathed.' Felix Porter, Twenty-Seven Elm Street, phone number 990-6888."

"Oh, I can give you a phone number, too," said Bookish Guy.

"Listen, would you both pipe down for a second?" said a see-through fireman floating about a foot off the ground, spirit orbs clustered around his head like bubbles. "I've got something really important I need to communicate here. It's about grease fires."

Norman looked around nervously. Because no one else could see or hear the ghosts, Norman would appear to be by the refreshment table chatting with himself. Which was fine, up to a point. But if his father noticed, he would most definitely get upset. Mr. Babcock hated it when Norman didn't act normal. And he almost never acted normal. *Para*normal was more like it.

"Bad mayo, no cat baths, got it," he murmured, holding a glass of orange punch in front of his face to disguise the movement of his lips.

"Well, my message is a little more complicated," said the fireman. "You'll probably want to take notes. Got a pen?"

"Let me go first, then," said the tallest, thinnest, baldest ghost Norman had ever seen. "There's a library book in my office, and I'm just not going to be able to get any eternal rest until someone takes it back."

Norman was reaching for a cookie to buy some time when he noticed something going on at the front door. A weird-looking man was trying to come in, and one of the dark-suited funeral-home guys was trying to keep him out. The man trying to come in was big and old-looking, his face covered by a bushy beard. He was wearing faded pants that were coming apart at the seams and an old green vest with several rips in it.

"I'm sorry, sir, but we do ask that visitors maintain a…certain dress code," the funeral-home guy was saying.

The weird man caught sight of Norman staring at him.

"Look, it's okay—all I want to do is talk to *him* for a minute," he said, pointing straight at Norman.

"Get in line, buster!" shouted Blue-Haired Lady. "Listen, kid, don't you have a cell phone or something? It's just one lousy phone call."

"You! I need to talk to you!" the man called from the door. He was looking kind of crazed. He didn't even have shoes on, just an old bag wrapped around each foot. What was this guy, some kind of nut job? Norman looked around the room nervously to see if people realized the nut job was addressing *him*.

The room was already mostly filled because it was a small town and everybody knew Grandma Babcock. Even Alvin was there, under the watchful eye of his terrifyingly thin grandmother. Norman pretended he didn't see Alvin. But Alvin sure saw him. And sure enough, half the town had stopped what they were doing to look around and see who was yelling in the doorway. And when they saw the crazy man pointing at Norman, they all turned and looked at Norman, too!

"No, *I* need to talk to him," shouted Bookish Guy, his spirit orbs dancing as if they were angry, too. "Buzz off, mister."

"Norman," began the crazy man.

Wait. How did this guy know his name?

"Do you have a cell phone?" asked Blue-Haired Lady.

"It's not even real mayonnaise; it's salad dressing," added Bookish Guy. "Can you just go over there and throw it in the garbage? She always leaves the back door unlocked."

"Listen, the book is called *Get Rich Knitting*. It's in my desk drawer. Okay?"

"Kid, where's your pen?" asked the fireman.

"Just hang on a second!" Norman exclaimed, still staring at the nutty-looking bearded man. Seriously, how *did* the guy know Norman's name? Could this be the crazy old uncle Mr. Babcock didn't want at the funeral?

"Sir, if you could please step away from the door," said the funeral-home director, looking distressed.

"I need that kid for one minute!" the man insisted. "You crazies clear out."

Norman blinked and then froze. Had the old man just talked...to the *ghosts*?

"Take a number!" shouted the ghost with glasses. "He's helping me stop a case of food poisoning!"

"No, he's helping me," insisted Blue-Haired Lady. "990-6888. Just call!"

"Look, public safety trumps the both of you, and this kid is helping me spread the word about how to put out grease fires!" hollered the fireman.

"I saw him first!" insisted the bald guy who wanted to get rich knitting.

Norman whirled around to face the line of ghosts.

"All of you just leave me alone! You have too many problems!" Norman bellowed at the top of his lungs.

The entire room fell silent. When he turned back around, every person there, dead and alive, was staring at Norman.

The only sound was Alvin's snorts of laughter. "Dude, you're the only one standing there! Who are you talking to, the vegetable dip?" he shouted before his grandmother shushed him.

Norman glowered at Alvin, but that only made him laugh harder.

The funeral-home guy gave the crazy man a discreet but powerful push backward and firmly closed the door. Over by one of the flower arrangements, Norman's father was hanging his head. Then he raised his eyes and looked right at his son. And although he didn't say anything, Norman knew exactly what he was thinking.

He had humiliated his father once again.

"Zombies can't talk—they mostly groan,"
Norman said.

Chapter Three

Norman sat quietly, observing the zombie as he stalked the perky teenage girl, his eye sockets glittering darkly and his smile crammed with broken, rotting teeth. Norman did not move from his spot on the floor next to the worn, sagging sofa even though he had seen this play out all too many times before. He knew the zombie was about to burst into the old cabin, where the girl was hiding. She was about to kick the bucket, and it wasn't going to be pretty.

"What's happening now?" came a voice behind him.

Norman's eyes remained glued to the television.

"The zombie is about to eat her head, Grandma," Norman told her.

One morning not long after her own funeral, Grandma Babcock had strolled into the living room right through a solid wall, as casually as if she'd just been down at the store getting a quart of milk. She'd been hanging around the house, mostly on the living room couch with Norman, ever since. It had been going on for about eleven months now, and she showed no signs of wanting to leave.

"That's not very nice," Grandma Babcock remarked. "What's he doing that for?"

"Because he's a zombie," Norman explained. "That's what they do."

"Well, he's going to ruin his jacket," Grandma Babcock observed. "I'm sure if they just bothered to sit down and talk it through, it'd be a whole different story."

"Zombies can't talk—they mostly groan," Norman said.

"Well, look at him. My goodness!" Grandma exclaimed as the camera zoomed in on the hideous leering face. "He looks like death on toast. What he needs to do is eat right, and take a little exercise. Maybe a nice power nap."

Norman chuckled. "He could use a rest, all right," he said. "A nice, eternal rest. He could—"

"Norman Babcock!" yelled a deep voice from the direction of the kitchen.

Norman winced.

"Didn't I tell you to take out the garbage?" the voice boomed.

Norman shot his grandmother an apologetic look as he got to his feet.

"Coming, Dad," he called.

It was really too bad—the zombie was just unhinging his jaw so he could get a really good bite of the teenager's skull. She was going to bleed like crazy. His father always interrupted during the good stuff.

Grandma Babcock gave Norman a look, squinting at him through her thick glasses and adjusting her pink-and-blue velour tracksuit.

"Tell him to turn up the thermostat, will ya?" she asked. "My feet are like ice."

Norman nodded and shuffled into the kitchen glumly.

"About time," Norman's dad grumbled. "Did you not hear the last twenty times I asked you to take out the trash? I was yelling loud enough to wake the dead."

Norman wordlessly opened the lid of the garbage can to tie up the bag. It *smelled* bad enough to wake the dead, too, he thought. And who was his dad trying to fool, all decked out in his Tool Town Professional Craftsman belt and safety goggles? He was changing a stupid lightbulb, for crud's sake.

"Thanks, sweetheart," his mother said, her back to him as she emptied the dishwasher. "You can get back to your show as soon as you toss that outside. Whaddya watching?"

"A movie about a zombie who eats brains," Norman said.

"That's nice," said his mother.

"But they have to be from living people," Norman added. "So the zombie has to bite their heads open while they're still alive."

"Sounds cute," his mom said, examining a spoon, then placing it back in the dishwasher.

Norman sighed and hauled the garbage bag out of the container.

"Zombies again?" his father muttered, pushing and pulling at the lightbulb with no visible result. "Why can't you be like other kids and pitch a tent in the yard in your free time, or save your allowance for a nice tool kit?"

"Because I like zombies," Norman said. *Because I like dead stuff in general*, he added silently. But he'd never say something like that out loud. In the eleven years he'd been on the planet, Norman had become something of an expert at flying under the radar, hiding his true personality. Oh, it was there, if you really looked. But no one ever did. Norman had learned early in life that all you had to do to avoid attention was to blend in, like wallpaper. But there was no disguising his love of zombie movies. One only had to walk into his room, which was covered with horror film posters and action figures and light-up zombie heads, to know that. Mr. Babcock stared at his son for a moment, then sighed and shook his head.

Grandma Babcock appeared in the doorway.

"Did you ask him about the thermostat?" she reminded Norman. "What in stars is he doing up there, anyway? Honestly. Tell him it's lefty loosey, righty tighty. Nothing's ever going to get done until he changes that stupid lightbulb."

Grandma Babcock stormed back to the living room. Norman stared at his father as he struggled with the light fixture.

"It's lefty loosey, righty tighty," he said.

Norman's dad stared at his son for a moment. Then he turned the lightbulb to the left. It popped neatly out of the socket. "Where'd you hear that?" he asked. "I haven't heard that expression in...oh man, Norman, the garbage is stinking up the whole house! What's wrong with you?"

"Maybe I should go shoplifting and joyriding like Courtney's friends?" Norman muttered under his breath, dragging the bag across the floor.

"Norman!" his mother said. "That isn't nice." Her sense of hearing was terrifyingly good sometimes.

Norman pushed open the back door with his foot as he hoisted the garbage bag up. Before he could carry it outside, something shot through the door. All Norman saw was a blur with blond hair and a cell phone, and a whiff of Crimson Cinnamon–scented lip gloss.

"Oh yeah, he is totally R-I-double-P-E-D! Like, a seven-pack at least! Norman, ew, you stink!"

Courtney reached out a perfectly pink manicured finger and poked Norman in the stomach.

"No, sorry, I was talking to my skunk-boy brother," Courtney said into her phone, wrinkling her nose to emphasize her disgust. "I know, right? I would if it were legal, or if I could get away with it."

"Courtney, be nice," Mrs. Babcock said automatically, still examining dishes and replacing them in the dishwasher.

Oh, I am being nice, Courtney thought. Really, her parents had no idea the personal and social costs of having Norman Babcock for a little brother. He was sooo weird. Who else in the known universe brushed his teeth with a zombie toothbrush while letting the toothpaste foam out of his mouth so he could pretend to be one of the walking dead, too? Courtney was positive she was already damaged for life just from having to share a bathroom with the kid.

Norman kicked open the screen door with his foot, walked several feet onto the back walkway, and hurled the plastic bag in the general direction of the garbage cans. Then he walked back inside, slamming the door behind him and heading for the living room, where he could hear the brain-nibbling zombie theme rising dramatically from the television set. He paused in the doorway that separated the living room from the kitchen.

"Oh, and, Dad? Grandma wants you to turn up the heat. Her feet are like ice."

Norman heard the clatter of a fork hitting the kitchen floor at the same moment his father jumped heavily off the ladder.

"Norman Babcock," his father said in his deepest, most newscaster voice.

Norman slowly turned to his father.

Of course, the easiest thing would have been to simply not pass along Grandma's request. But she had specifically asked. To ignore her would have been just rude. Life seemed complicated enough without having to resort to *that*.

"Okay, I know that *you* know that your grandmother is dead," Mr. Babcock said.

Norman scowled.

"Yep," he said.

"Then why do you insist on talking to her?" Mr. Babcock asked sharply, dropping the new lightbulb he'd just unwrapped. The bulb made an ominous tinkling sound when it hit the floor and shattered.

"Because," Norman replied slowly, "she talks back!"

Courtney snapped her phone shut and gave her brother what she thought was a withering look.

"OMG, you are such a little liar," she drawled.

"I am not," Norman retorted. "She asks me stuff all the time. She tells me stuff, too."

Courtney rolled her eyes so wildly, she threw herself off balance a little. She kicked off both of her hot-pink sneakers, plopped down at the kitchen table, and locked eyes with her brother.

"Oh yeah?" she challenged. "Prove it!"

Norman returned her steely gaze. He did not like to flaunt his connection with the underworld, which gave him access to all kinds of information that could, if in the wrong hands, really flip people out. But the subject had come up now, and Courtney was asking for it. To be fair, she was practically begging.

"Well, Grandma says you have pictures of the varsity football quarterback with his shirt off hidden in your underwear drawer," he told her.

Courtney's face instantly turned crimson with fury as she leaped to her feet. Nobody was supposed to know that. If word got out in school, her life would be ruined. She would have to move to another state. Probably another country!

"You disgusting, spying little *creep!*" she exploded, flouncing out of the kitchen, her blond ponytail bobbing furiously behind her.

Norman was left with the dual images of his mother, who looked dismayed and a bit angry and was hiding it with a smile, and his father, who looked angry and a bit dismayed and was hiding it with a scowl.

"Sweetie, the important thing is that Grandma's in a better place now," his mother began.

Norman felt that if it were possible for a human to fly into bits from sheer frustration, he was going to do it right then. How could he be related to any of these people? By what mutation of science did any of them share his DNA?

"A better place?" his father mocked. "We all know where Grandma is, Sandra. For Pete's sake, why don't we all start by just calling it what it is?"

"The living room?" asked Norman.

Then he turned on his heel and walked away before either of his parents could react.

Norman watched the rest of the movie with Grandma Babcock partly because she needed him to explain parts of it to her and partly because he really loved the scene at the end when the rest of the zombies came lurching out of the graveyard and chartered a schooner and set sail on the high seas to begin their new careers as zombie pirates. That bit just never got old.

When the credits began to roll, he wished Grandma Babcock good night and walked up the stairs, wondering, as he sometimes did, where she went when she wasn't somewhere Norman could see her.

At least she stays out of my room most of the time, Norman thought, sitting wearily on the edge of his bed. *I wouldn't want her poking around in* my *underwear drawer.* Though the most exciting thing anyone was liable to find there was Norman's *Revenge of the Zombies* action-figure set.

It had been a very long day. Between the toad and Alvin and Neil trying to get him to stick out less and Salma trying to persuade him to improve his study habits, and the usual fun with the folks and big sis Courtney, Norman felt like he'd been squeezed through a car wash, then sucked up in a giant vacuum cleaner and spat back out again.

"Who cares if I sleep in my clothes?" he asked his *Portals of Peril* poster. When there was no response, Norman shoved off the books and clothes that had been piled on his bed and got under the covers.

From the ancient heating vents that snaked through the entire house, Norman could hear his parents' voices in a hushed and familiar conversation. His father's voice was louder than his mother's, and snippets of his remarks floated into Norman's ears.

"People talk, Sandra. Everybody knows he isn't normal."

His mother said something in a low voice that Norman couldn't make out.

"No, Sandra, you want to know what's crazy? That

uncle of yours. And I'm worried maybe Norman's got what *he* got."

More mumbling from Mrs. Babcock.

"I'm the man, and I'm telling you right now 'sensitive' is writing poetry and not doing sports. What Norman's got is way worse than sensitive."

Norman sighed and pulled the pillow over his head.

Norman and his dad had never exactly been best buddies, not like the fathers and sons you saw on television commercials for sporting-goods stores or build-your-own-telescope kits. But ever since the incident at the funeral home, it had been like this. His father just couldn't accept who Norman was. Really, none of his family could.

There came a point when Norman realized that if an entire town thought you were headed for the funny farm, there was no sense in pretending otherwise. That was why, after his grandmother died, Norman took the very uncomplicated step of acting exactly like the person he was. And that meant talking to people and pets and other things that had recently or not so recently departed the earth. He did it quietly, but he did it.

As a result, most people were not very comfortable around Norman. And no one was more not comfortable than Mr. Babcock, particularly after word of the funeral-home incident spread like wildfire through Blithe Hollow.

"Whatever," mumbled Norman, turning onto his side and pulling the pillow off his head so he could get a bit of air.

A translucent moth was hovering around the head of the bed. Tiny spirit orbs no bigger than pinheads swirled near the moth's wings.

"Hi," Norman said.

The moth seemed to look at Norman, though it was hard to tell for sure. Then it flew really fast over to the lamp next to Norman's bed, circled it a few times, then flew back toward Norman.

"What?" Norman asked.

The moth flew back to the lamp again, hovered there a moment, then dashed back.

"Oh, I think I get it," Norman said. Then he reached up and turned on the light. Happy now, the phantom moth fluttered around the lightbulb.

"No problem," Norman murmured. Then he fluffed his pillows a few times and got comfortable, leaving the light on so the dead moth could enjoy it.

"She summoned them to return as the *living dead*, to wander Blithe Hollow terrifying the innocent, doomed to an *eternity* of DAMNATION!"

Chapter Four

That night, Norman dreamed of the strange man from the funeral home. In the dream, the man was standing in a dark room cluttered with junk, clutching an old leather book with an illustration on the cover of an ethereal wisp of a woman sleeping beneath a scattering of stars. The man seemed to be sick, or hurt. He dropped the book and doubled over in pain.

Norman caught a glimpse of a desk in one corner of the room. The desk was covered with photographs. Photographs of *Norman*. In one of them, he was standing on the beach with his family, and he was circled with *red ink*.... Then Norman woke up.

"Wow!" Norman said, sitting straight up in bed. "That was freaky."

He could smell Cherry Frosted Toaster Cakes being warmed up downstairs, but Norman didn't feel like interacting with his family this morning. The dream had sort of taken the wind out of his sails, and it was only 7:30. He decided to linger upstairs. He spent a full three minutes standing in his zombie slippers, brushing his teeth with the matching zombie toothbrush, letting the foam spill out of his mouth until he looked demented and possibly rabid. Then he changed the alarm on his tombstone clock from CACKLE to HOWL. He spent a long time rearranging some of his movie posters so that the *Brain Eater* one was more visible, since it was his current favorite. Norman's plan was to stay in his room killing time until the very last minute, then rush out the door for school. But he dawdled for too long—the kitchen was empty and even Courtney had already left. That meant he was later than usual. Norman sped down the street. He hated being late.

• ◆ •

Just before the bridge that led into town, Norman spied a woman in an old-timey leather flight suit and custom-made goggles swinging from a parachute that was entwined in the branches of a huge oak tree.

"Morning, Harriet, how's it hanging?" Norman called.

"Hah, never heard that one before. Don't give up your day job, kid!"

"I won't," Norman called, heading over the bridge. "I'll try to swing by again on my way home."

Harriet hooted. Like many of the ghosts Norman saw on his walk to school, Harriet didn't want anything. She'd been hanging around that old tree, where she'd ended her earthly life as a skydiving heiress, just because she seemed to like taking risks. A simple "good morning" was all that many of Blithe Hollow's spirits really needed.

As he crossed the bridge, Norman was looking over his shoulder at a turn-of-the-century raven that was perched on the railing cawing when he almost collided with a shimmering horse.

"As you were, soldier," called a bedraggled and overly bandaged man in a dirty blue uniform from atop the horse.

"Sorry, sir!"

"Look lively, young greenhorn!" the soldier barked. "Word is, President Lincoln is making a big announcement today!"

Norman waved and started walking faster. He did not stop to chat with Hippie Guy, Greaser Ghost, or the handsome Native American warrior who wore huge beaded earrings in both ears. He hurried up Main Street past Hair Dryer Lady, who was in an eternal battle with the cowlick on the left side of her head, and right by Crossing Guard Man, who carried a crumpled stop sign and had tire tracks running right across his bright green vest, and who, as usual, was not watching the traffic or the pedestrians at all (which explained a lot).

Maybe Norman was just in a bad mood, but it seemed to him that Blithe Hollow was looking even more tired and run-down than usual today. What could you expect from a place that created an entire identity for itself out of a witchcraft trial? And with the three hundredth anniversary of the trial fast approaching, it seemed like the entire town had lost its collective mind with excitement. The anniversary was apparently the most exciting thing to happen in Blithe Hollow since the trial itself.

"Hey, how you doin'?" asked a shimmering man in a beautiful camel-hair coat and black fedora hat, cradling an oversize machine gun under one arm.

"How *you* doin'?" Norman asked Mobster Dude automatically, looking both ways as he crossed Main Street.

"Cheese it, it's the cops!" Mobster Dude called after him. The ghost tried to run away, but his feet were stuck in a concrete block.

Norman glanced up the street at the odd couple of Sheriff Hooper, who was dark-skinned, round, and matronly, and Deputy Dwayne, who was tall, pale, and skinny. They appeared to be arguing over who was going to write out a parking ticket. Unlike everyone else Norman had seen so far, the sheriff and the deputy were not see-through. They were one hundred percent alive, though you wouldn't always know it by watching them "working."

Norman trotted down the sidewalk toward the end of Main Street. As usual, he found the sight of the town center depressing. Run-down signs advertised THE CAULDRON CAFÉ, BEWITCHED IN BLITHE, and the risky barbershop, TRICK OR TRIM. A massive billboard in the main square was festooned with a cheerful cartoon of a witch swinging from the gallows while a hangman next to her waved, and enormous orange lettering read BLITHE HOLLOW—A GREAT PLACE TO HANG! Every business in town was trying to somehow play off the witch theme. Strung up over the street between a coffee shop called The Brew and a greeting-card store named Best

• 37 •

Witches was a huge banner advertising the most important thing to happen in the town for centuries: the anniversary of the famous trial. BLITHE HOLLOW—300 BEWITCHIN' YEARS!, the sign bragged.

"Man, that is so pathetic," Norman mumbled to himself.

There was a squeak and a chittering chirp in response.

Norman looked down at the street and saw a raccoon that had apparently been on the losing end of a disagreement with a motor vehicle.

"Oh, hey there," Norman said, bending down to greet the animal. "I didn't see you at first. You're new."

The raccoon sort of shrugged and shook its head. It pointed at the corner where there was no stop sign in place.

"Yeah, there used to be a sign there," Norman explained, looking around. "I think someone hit it, though."

A man coming out of The Brew saw Norman talking to roadkill and gave him a strange look, shaking his head and deliberately walking backward to go in the opposite direction.

"Whatever," Norman murmured, turning left down the street that led to a squat brick building behind an ugly granite marker reading BLITHE HOLLOW MIDDLE SCHOOL. Only a few kids were still heading through the main door, so Norman knew he really was late. As he hurried toward the stairs, Norman thought he caught a glimpse of someone in a dark coat standing beside an old dead tree down the street. Whoever it was withdrew from sight—maybe it was a new ghost who hadn't figured Norman out yet. There'd be time to look into that later.

Norman hurried up the stairs and through the school's entrance. Before he had taken two steps into the hallway, someone knocked him to the ground.

"Excuse you," Norman muttered, getting back to his feet. Some lug-heads in lacrosse jerseys stood there, watching him and snickering. Norman ignored them and made his way to his locker, pulling out an old rag from his pocket even before getting close enough to see the word FREAK written in lipstick right above his yellow combination lock. Apparently, Alvin and his Meaty Henchmen were getting an early start today.

"Morning," came a cheerful, squeaky voice.

Norman glanced over at Neil Downe, who spritzed a bottle of Schmutz B Gone on his locker and then started wiping off the word FATTY.

"Hey, Neil," Norman said. "Um, can I borrow your cleaner?"

Neil handed Norman the bottle. "It's actually Salma's," he said. "Somebody wrote *Dorkula* on her locker in green crayon."

"Thanks," Norman said, squirting the stuff over the red letters and wiping them off. "I've gotta go to math now."

"There is no math today," came a voice behind Norman as he opened his locker. He turned to see Salma, her glossy black hair pulled into a painfully tight–looking ponytail and her braces gleaming in the fluorescent lights. She extended her hand, and Norman handed her the bottle.

"Special pageant rehearsal, remember?" she asked.

Neil groaned. "Noooo," he complained.

"It's required," Salma declared. "If you skip it, it goes on your permanent record. This isn't just any pageant; it's the three hundredth anniversary pageant. Mrs. Henscher is totally obsessed."

Neil obediently followed Salma down the hall, and after a moment, Norman slammed his locker shut and went, too.

The gym smelled of used sneakers and ancient

rubber, which was somehow more difficult to stomach in the morning. At the opposite end of the room from the old metal bleachers was a small stage, strewn with bad art-class representations of Colonial life and framed with plywood hills painted a dubious slime green, a lopsided chapel, and a crescent moon that hung perilously from the basketball hoop.

"We have no dignity in this school," Norman mumbled to himself, just as the theater teacher, Mrs. Henscher, swept by and handed him an enormous papier-mâché Pilgrim hat. Alvin and his Meaty Henchmen were huddled on the bleachers, pointing at Norman and squealing with laughter.

"Nice hat, ghooost boy," sang Alvin. "Where's your frog friend today?"

The horror.

"People, pick up a script from the pile and take your places," Mrs. Henscher shrieked. She was a large, imposing woman who wore glasses just for show and, to emphasize her position as the director, a tiny red beret that flopped on her head like a deflated balloon. Everyone was terrified of Mrs. Henscher. She looked like a linebacker in a wig, her fleshy, moon-shaped face dwarfing her undersized mouth and dark beady eyes. She wore shapeless black pants that barely covered her bulk and were yanked up high over her considerable stomach. When she shouted, which was a lot of the time, her face and body quivered with the booming vibration like a kiddie pool in an earthquake. Nobody with any brains got in Mrs. Henscher's way when she was excited about something. And right now, all she cared about was her pageant. She had cast Norman as Narrator #1.

The humiliation.

Norman would rather go six rounds in the cafeteria with Alvin than read Mrs. Henscher's schlocky script out loud. But he had enough dubious stuff on his permanent record already. Plopping the hat onto his head, he walked over to the stage, where Salma was already waiting. She was wearing a black pointy witch's hat, and not to throw stones while living in a glass house or anything, but Norman couldn't help thinking she looked stupid. Salma might have agreed, since she was attempting to argue with Mrs. Henscher about her costume. She was the only person Norman had ever seen who wasn't afraid to question the teacher.

"...clearly contemporary sources confirm that people accused of witchcraft looked extremely normal, and the idea of green skin and a broomstick are completely apocryphal and are really more an indication of our collective cultural obsession with *The Wizard of Oz* than an accurate reflection of..." Salma was saying.

Mrs. Henscher all but stuck her fingers in her ears. "Salma, for heaven's sake, stop your prattling. Now, people, remember that Pilgrims were strict and devout settlers who came to Blithe Hollow to make a new home for themselves. Try to remember that. We are starting from the top of page six, please."

Norman held the script in front of his face and read in the flattest monotone he could muster. "The founding fathers of Blithe Hollow learned to their everlasting horror that there was an evil witch among them."

"No, no, *stop!*" Mrs. Henscher cried, grabbing Norman's script from his hand. "You must do it *thus.*"

She cleared her throat. "They discovered, to their eeeeever-*last*-ing horr-*or*"—here Mrs. Henscher's voice rose to such a shriek that Norman imagined fine crystal shattering halfway across the county—"an eeeeevil *witch* among them!"

Now she began to wave her arms around hysterically.

"They put the evil creature on trial, then hanged her from an old, dying tree—but the vengeful, foul witch *cursed* the seven brave Pilgrims as she died, condemning them to a *fate worse than death*! For that vile sorceress did cause them to perish in soul but not in body, and she summoned them to return as the *living dead,* to wander Blithe Hollow terrifying the innocent, doomed to an *eternity* of DAMNATION!"

Mrs. Henscher's beret flew off as she bellowed the final line, spraying the stage with spit as she overpronounced every syllable. Then she handed the script back to Norman.

"Got that?" she asked.

"Um..." he said, but he took the script back because anything would be better than listening to Mrs. Henscher read the lines again.

Then, just for a moment, something really strange happened.

Now, Norman was used to all kinds of strange, but this was something he had never experienced before. As he stood staring at the script, the paper turned yellow and parchmentlike before his eyes. His head went funny and swimmy, and he lost his balance and took a step backward. The other cast members on the stage seemed to fade into blurs, and when they came back into focus momentarily, they were...not themselves anymore. They were other people altogether. Seven people. Gone were the tacky dime-store Thanksgiving costumes—these were tall, shimmering figures in real Pilgrim clothes. It was as if he had been momentarily transported back in time.

All the blood rushed to Norman's head, and he dropped the script as little black spots began dancing in front of his eyes.

I'm going to faint, Norman thought, just as his legs gave way, and he sat down hard on the stage.

The world came back in a snap, led by the nauseating sound of Alvin's Hyena Laugh.

"Normie fell down and go boom, baby! Look at him! He's white as a sheet! Whassamatter, Norm, you look like you *saw a ghost*! Get it? Get it? A ghost!"

The laughter of Alvin and his Meaty Henchmen was momentarily drowned out by the sound of the bell. Leaving his script where it had fallen, Norman jumped to his feet and sped out of the gym.

For just a moment, he was the only person in the hallway—everything looked oddly deserted and devoid of human life.

Like how a school might look in a ghost town.

"Did that statue just say 'psssst'?"
asked Neil.

Chapter Five

It was always such a relief to get out of school. Norman looked forward all day to the moment when he could finally get away from the other kids. He slung his book bag over one shoulder and began to walk down the sidewalk. But as he walked, he kept hearing an echo of his footsteps. No—not *his* footsteps. Somebody else's.

Someone was following Norman.

Norman shifted his bag onto the other shoulder, and without looking back, he began walking much faster. The footsteps sped up to match his. He wasn't just being followed.

He was being chased.

Norman came to a sudden stop and spun around, ready to defend himself against Alvin or whatever hideous thing had him in its sights.

Neil Downe was right at his elbow, his face bright with a friendly grin.

"Oh. Neil," Norman said. "Look, I already told you, I like to be alone."

"Me too," Neil said. "That's what makes it perfect. We can be alone together!"

Norman started walking again. Really fast. His backpack bounced on his hip.

Neil started trotting to keep up with Norman. "Come on, it'd be fun." Then he added conspiratorially, "You know, Alvin bothers me, too."

"Why?" Norman asked in spite of himself. He knew that he shouldn't ask questions if he was trying to end a conversation. Not with dead people, and certainly not with Neil.

"Because I'm fat. I have wicked allergies. I sweat when I walk too fast. I have irritable bowel syndrome, and I get hives whenever I see a long-division problem. And that's just for starters."

Norman slowed down for a moment and examined Neil's slightly flushed face. Neil did sweat a little when he walked fast, and his hair was weird, and irritable bowel syndrome sounded bad under any circumstances. But Norman also noticed how clear and bright Neil's eyes were.

He's probably a pretty good guy, Norman suddenly thought.

"You shouldn't let Alvin and his friends get to you," Norman told him.

"Oh, I don't, usually," Neil said. "Bullying is part of human nature. If you were bigger and a lot more stupid, you might be a bully, too. It's called 'survival of the thickest.'"

Norman was about to argue that there was no known force on earth that could cause him to act like Alvin even for a second when something caught his eye.

He and Neil were standing near one of the ugliest sights in Blithe Hollow—the town square featured a modern bronze statue that was supposed to be the evil witch of local lore. To Norman, it looked like something a cat had coughed up. He usually tried to avoid looking at it, but right now Norman was getting the impression that something or some*one* was hiding behind it. He stopped to examine it more closely. Neil did, too.

"Did that statue just say 'psssst'?" asked Neil.

Norman certainly thought so. There was something there, but it didn't have a dead-thing vibe. And Neil had heard it, too, so whatever was going on, Norman knew it didn't involve the supernatural. Suddenly, something leaped out in front of them.

"You. Boy. You know who I am?" it wheezed.

Norman and Neil both took a step backward.

A hulking man stood hunched over with age and rage, scowling at the two of them, his dark clothes ragged and unwashed. A wild, thick beard covered half his face, his old green vest was in tatters, and in place of shoes he had an old bag around each foot, tied at the ankle with twine.

"The weird, stinky old bum who lives out by the graveyard?" Neil asked. "The crypt keeper?"

The old man pointed at Norman.

"I'm talking to *you*," he said.

"I know who you are," Norman said, trying to take another step back without giving the appearance that he was running away. Nobody had actually talked to him about it after the funeral, but Norman had heard things.

"I'm not supposed to talk to you," Norman said.

"Why not?" Neil asked. "Other than the crypt-keeper thing?"

The old man glowered.

"Because I can see ghosts, too," he growled. "Just like you, Norman Babcock. It's getting worse, isn't it? You're seeing more of them everywhere. You're starting to have bad dreams, sinister visions. Faces peering through the veil!"

"I . . . there isn't . . . how do you . . ." Norman's voice faltered. He glanced at Neil, who was staring at the old man with his mouth slightly open.

"This is the dark secret of Blithe Hollow, the shameful untold legend of the witch's curse," the old man hissed.

"Oh, it's not a secret," Neil said.

"Actually, we're learning about it," explained Norman.

"We're doing a play about it in school right now," added Neil. "For the three hundredth anniversary. I'm a tree!"

Norman and the old man both shot Neil a look. Norman's look was supposed to communicate "Please do not say anything else."

The old man took a step closer to Norman.

"There is something you must know before the anniversary is upon us," he whispered. "The most important thing you will ever hear—the fate of every man, woman, and child in Blithe Hollow depends upon it! The witch's curse is very real, and on the eve of the three hundredth anniversary of her death, the veil between your two worlds will drop away and her rage will know no bounds unless you use your power to speak to the dead. Unless you stop her, Norman Babcock!"

"Whoa," said Neil.

"Come on," Norman said, grabbing Neil's arm. "We gotta go."

Prenderghast. That was the name of the crazy old great-uncle whom Norman had been told repeatedly to stay away from. That crazy guy who had shouted at him in the funeral home. The man he'd seen in his dream. Norman did not know why his parents were so insistent that Norman not speak with his great-uncle. But Mr. Prenderghast gave him a very, very bad feeling.

Norman tried to take another giant step back, but this time, Mr. Prenderghast reached out and grabbed his sleeve with one bony hand.

"Listen to me," he said. "You must go to the grave-yard and—"

The old man's voice was interrupted by an ugly cough that caused him to double over, his face beet red and his eyes bulging. Norman tried to squirm away, but the old man had the grip of death on him.

"Let him go!" squeaked Neil. Norman caught a glimpse of Neil rummaging around in his kitten lunch box. Then an apple flew through the air and bounced off Mr. Prenderghast's head, causing him to lose his grip on Norman's sleeve.

"Come on!" yelled Neil, grabbing Norman's arm.

The two of them ran up the street like a couple of spooked deer.

"I'm not done with you, Babcock!" the old man yelled. "You must watch for the sign!"

Norman and Neil didn't stop until they reached the bridge to the Babcocks' side of town. They stood together, breathing heavily and casting glances up the street to make sure the old man hadn't followed them.

"Geez, what a nutty old creep," Neil said. "What sewer did he crawl out of, do you figure?"

"He's actually my great-uncle," Norman said.

"For real?" Neil asked.

Norman nodded.

"Well, I have an uncle who's in jail 'cause he stole from nuns," Neil said with a dismissive shrug. "So is it true? Do you really talk to dead people?"

Oh, here we go, Norman thought. For a minute there, he'd almost enjoyed Neil's company. But now Norman had been asked The Question, and once he gave a straight answer, Neil would fall all over himself running away.

"Yeah, it's true," Norman said, sounding more defensive than he'd meant to.

"Awesome. Does that include dogs, by any chance? I miss Bub—he was a good dog. Will you come over to my house and try to find him?"

Norman stared at Neil. Had Neil misunderstood him?

"I said yes. I *do* talk to the dead," he clarified.

"Right—cool!" Neil said enthusiastically. "So would you just come to my yard? Have a peek? See if Bub's around?"

Norman did not know what to say. Was Neil a little soft in the head? Nobody had ever thought it was cool that Norman talked to the dearly departed.

But Neil was already heading in the direction of his house. After thinking about it for a moment, Norman caught up with him.

"My house is just up here," Neil said.

"Neil, I'm not sure you—" Norman began.

"Hey, no pressure," Neil said. "If you see him, great. If not, no big deal. Here it is."

Neil pulled Norman up the driveway of an olive-colored house with brownish-reddish shutters. It was much better cared for than the houses on either side of it, which drooped and peeled like the average Blithe Hollow home.

In the driveway was parked a tricked-out old van, beneath which protruded a long pair of muscular legs.

"Who's that? Neil?" called a voice from beneath the camper. "Bro? That you?"

"Hey, Mitch. You're stuck again, aren't you?" Neil said. He nudged Norman with one elbow and grinned.

"I'm not...I just—yeah, I'm stuck, okay?" came the voice. "My shirt is caught on the pointy thing. Just get me outta here, will ya?"

Neil bent down and grabbed both of Mitch's ankles. He gave one mighty tug, and Mitch shot out from beneath the van.

"Ow. Ow!" Mitch yelled.

"You're welcome," Neil said. "This is Norman. We're going into the yard to play with Bub."

Mitch sat on the pavement rubbing one arm. He was a strapping, powerful-looking guy, at least six feet tall, by Norman's reckoning. The only thing he had in common with Neil was the red hair. But on Mitch, it actually looked good.

"Uh, Neil?" Mitch said, getting to his feet. "Can you come here a second?"

Mitch wrapped one muscled arm around Neil's shoulders without waiting for a response and led him a few feet away while Norman awkwardly pretended to admire the cheerful lawn ornaments festooning the front walkway. The one with the polka-dotted ladies' bloomers was particularly colorful. But he also liked the pink flamingos next to the red dragon mailbox.

Norman heard a few phrases. "That weird kid" and "pretends to see ghosts" and "not a good dude to hang out with."

"Cut it out, Mitch," Norman heard Neil say. "He's no weirder than I am. Actually, he's just as weird as I am. I like him."

Neil ducked out from beneath Mitch's arm and gestured to Norman.

"Come on," he said. "Bub liked to hang out around back."

Exchanging a quick, uncomfortable look with Mitch, Norman followed Neil around to the back of the house, where he instantly caught sight of a dog prancing on the perfectly manicured lawn.

"So, what, can you see him?" Neil asked. "Is he there?"

The dog was there, all right, all of him. Twice. Which is to say there was a front half, and a back half. They just didn't happen to be connected.

"How did your dog die, Neil?" asked Norman.

"The animal-rescue van ran over him," Neil said. "It was tragically ironic. So can you see him? How does he look?"

Norman hesitated a moment, then he took the plunge. He told Neil exactly what he saw and waited for Neil to freak out and ask him to leave.

But all Neil wanted was for Norman to help him figure out how to play fetch with Bub in his new, split-through-the-middle form.

So Norman did—not because Bub wanted his help, or because he felt like he had to, but for the simple, odd reason that Neil was good company.

And for the first time in as long as he could remember, Norman was having fun.

"The dead are coming,"
whispered the tree.

Chapter Six

Norman was tired out from the afternoon of phantom fetch with Neil and Bub. Neil had way more energy than Norman would have guessed, and they had played almost until dinnertime. Mr. Feynman had piled on the homework, and Norman still had lines to learn for the pageant. The performance was only two days away. Now it was getting late, and he just didn't have the energy for a scholastic skirmish with Salma.

"But if we're going to be lab partners, I have to be sure you have a workable understanding of the apparatus," Salma was saying. "And not just structurally, but cognitively and perceptually. Norman? Norman?"

Norman brought the phone back to his ear with a start.

"Sorry. I kind of nodded off."

"That's not the kind of cognitive and perceptual I was looking for—"

"Salma, can I talk to you in school about this? I need to sleep. Things are kind of . . . stressed for me right now."

Salma sighed. As a near-perfect student with parents who complained if there was no + after her *A*, and as a person who received more than her fair share of torture from Alvin and his Meaty Henchmen, she could relate to Norman's use of the word *stress*.

"Okay, we'll talk tomorrow," she said. "Get some rest."

Norman almost fell asleep right there at his desk. But he managed to stagger over to his bed, zombie style, and fall face-first onto the pillow without even taking off his shoes.

Unfortunately, his sleep was anything but stress-free. He began to dream of Mr. Prenderghast again.

In the dream, the old man was pacing in a decrepit old study crammed full of junk, panting and wheezing and muttering to himself.

"Thinks he can hide behind his weird little fat friend, does he? I'll show him. He can't pretend I don't exist anymore."

Mr. Prenderghast rummaged through a stack of papers piled high on an old desk. He grabbed an old leather book with a familiar cover showing a young woman beneath a scattering of stars.

"Here it is. He'll take it whether he likes it or not, stupid little punk. Doesn't he realize we're running out of time?"

In the dream, Norman viewed this entire scene as if he were standing right there in the room with Mr. Prenderghast. The whole thing had a strange, super-realistic quality to it, like Norman had wandered into a documentary inside a huge TV.

Suddenly, Mr. Prenderghast gave a strange croak, clutched the book to his chest, yelled "Not yet!" and then dropped to the ground like a stone. Almost immediately, a stream of spectral ghost orbs sputtered out of his body, re-creating his shape in translucent light, a shape that then staggered to his feet.

"Aw, nuts," snapped the ghost of Mr. Prenderghast. "I've kicked the bucket."

Norman opened his eyes for a moment and had just enough time awake to think, *What a weird, messed-up dream.* And then he was asleep again.

This time, he had a more regular dream. He was standing onstage during the opening scene of the pageant, and he could not remember his lines. Mrs. Henscher was yelling at him, and everybody in the audience was laughing, and Norman could see Alvin and Mitch in the front row, hooting and pointing. He looked down and realized he'd accidentally walked out onstage wearing only his underwear.

Great.

• ◆ •

Before the actual performance of the anniversary pageant two nights later, Norman remembered his dream, and while he stood backstage, he checked carefully to make sure he had on all of his costume. The seats were packed, and Mrs. Henscher was buzzing around, barking orders at people. Neil and Salma were going over some lines by the little watercooler, but Norman did not join them. He did not feel like talking until he had to. When Mrs. Henscher began hissing "Places, everyone!" Norman knew his quiet time was up. *Might as well just get this over with, and then I can go home*, Norman thought. *No problem.* But he was wrong about that. From that moment on, things went hideously and embarrassingly wrong, even by Norman's standards.

The lights came up on Norman, who stood squinting out at the audience for a moment, his eyes gradually focusing enough to make out the figures of his parents fiddling with a video camera in the front row. Fortunately, he had no lines yet. That burden fell on Salma, and because she had a photographic memory, Norman wasn't too worried for her. At the opposite end of the stage stood Neil, framed in an enormous Styrofoam construction of black and brown limbs that was supposed to be a tree.

Salma stood center stage in her ridiculous witch costume, which made her look more like a guest villain on a cartoon than a historical figure. The kids playing the six Pilgrim jurors and the judge stood in a semicircle around her. They had just condemned Salma's witch character to death and were grinning cheerfully and waiting for her to get through her big moment so they could kill her.

"I curse you!" Salma yelled, baring her braces as she grimaced at her accusers. "You shall die a horrible and gruesome death, then rise from your graves as the living dead! I doom your souls to an eternity of damnation, and your bodies to everlasting mortification!"

Norman took a deep breath. The seven Pilgrims were supposed to chant "Kill the witch" for a while, and then there would be a light change, after which Salma would sneak offstage and be presumed dead, because you couldn't actually show that stuff. That's when Norman was supposed to start speaking. As the seven began to chant, Norman heard the unmistakable voice of his mother squeal, "Perry, aren't they all adorable?" And then Norman heard something else. A low hooting sound.

Norman looked up and saw an owl with large glowing eyes staring at him from a beam near the gymnasium ceiling. Was he hallucinating? What was an enormous owl doing up there—how could it have gotten inside? Maybe the lights were messing with his eyes. Norman blinked, then looked at the floor, then back up at the ceiling. The owl was still there. It hooted again, then spread its wings and glided across the stage, right over the astonished Norman's head. The owl landed on one of Neil's Styrofoam branches. Neil caught Norman's confused look and raised his eyebrows in a silent "What's wrong?" *Is Neil blind?*

The sounds of the Pilgrim chorus chanting "Kill the witch" began to sound muffled, as if someone had dropped an enormous pillow onstage. Norman's vision went all funny. The shapes of the chorus and the audience went out of focus, blurred as if a finger had smudged them. The ceiling of the gym disintegrated into a cloud-filled sky that crackled with lightning.

"Uh-oh," Norman whispered.

The gym, the stage, even Salma and Neil, were gone.

Norman was standing in a dark forest in the middle of a storm. Wind howled through the branches and lightning cracked in the sky. Through the thick tree trunks, he could glimpse little dots of yellow light in the distance. He knew he was in the oldest part of the woods, near Knob Hill, just outside of town.

Norman heard the sound of something thrashing around in the undergrowth behind him.

"Witch! Come on out! We're going to find you!" yelled a man's voice.

Norman froze, his heart beating wildly.

"Witch!" shrieked a woman's voice. "We're coming for you!"

Norman heard branches snapping. Then, suddenly, a woman burst through the trees just in front of him. She was wearing the dark, drab outfit of a Pilgrim— and this was no costume. Strands of her hair had come loose, and her eyes were hysterical and wide. She stopped dead in her tracks when she caught sight of Norman. He shook his head, giving her a silent, pleading look.

"The witch is here!" yelled the woman. "I've found the witch!"

Norman's insides turned to jelly.

"No," he tried to say, but nothing but a gasp came out of his mouth. More branches snapped, and then two men pushed through the brush and appeared next to the woman. They were carrying pitchforks and torches, and one had a coil of rope over his shoulder.

"Die, witch!" one of the men shouted.

Norman yelled with fright and spun around, running blindly in the other direction. He took seven or eight steps before crashing face-first into the rough trunk of a massive old tree. In the center of the trunk was a twisted knothole that gaped like a mouth.

"The dead are coming," whispered the tree.

Norman yelled again, smacking at the tree with his hands, but was afraid to turn and face his pursuers.

"Norman? Are you okay?" He suddenly heard a familiar voice coming from the tree.

Norman blinked rapidly, his hands still pushing against the tree. But the bark had become softer suddenly, and in the place where the knothole had been, a familiar face came into focus. Neil Downe was peeking out of the old tree, his red eyebrows knit with concern.

"Is something wrong?" Neil asked.

And before he could stop himself, Norman answered. And he didn't just speak; he bellowed. Right there in front of Neil and Salma and his parents and pretty much half of Blithe Hollow, Norman Babcock threw his head back and yelled as loudly as he could.

"The dead are coming!"

• ◆ •

There was really no way to salvage the situation after that. Norman had grown accustomed to freaking people out, but this was pushing the limit even for him. Shoving Neil out of the way, Norman tried to run behind a backdrop, but he'd gotten turned around in the forest vision and instead plummeted straight off the stage. He landed with a thwack on the gymnasium floor in front of a familiar pair of shoes in the first row of the audience.

"This is all part of the play, right, Norman? Tell me this is *all part of the play*, son!" came a slightly hysterical voice.

"Norman, my goodness! Are you hurt?" he heard his mother exclaim.

"Dude, did you say the *dead* are coming?" called out another voice. This one sounded suspiciously like Mitch, the overly muscled brother of Neil.

"Who said the dead are coming?" asked someone else, and then the voices blended together in a mass babble. A hint of actual fear began to ripple through the crowd.

Norman stood up and faced the audience defiantly.

"Yes, the dead *are* coming." Faces turned to listen to Norman, and then he explained. "The tree told me!"

In terms of pure logic, it was not the best argument Norman could have made. He looked over at Neil in his silly tree costume. But Neil's face was red, and he was looking down at the floor. He sort of shook his head a little.

The audience erupted in gales of laughter. Mr. Babcock stood up quickly and grabbed Norman by the arm.

"We're leaving," he snapped. "All of us. Sandra, let's go."

Norman allowed his father to drag him from the gymnasium because he really saw no advantage in staying behind. He looked over his shoulder long enough to register the bewildered faces of Neil and Salma onstage. So much for thinking about having friends. Then everything was a blur until the door slammed behind him, and the cool night air in the parking lot made him feel, finally, that he might not be losing his mind.

"Norman, have you lost your mind?" his father snapped, unlocking the car with a grim look on his face.

"No," Norman said, but his father talked right over him.

"It's one thing acting like a mental case in the privacy of your own home, but this was in front of half the freakin' town! And just when they were starting to forget what happened at your grandma's funeral! Let's get something straight right now, Norman Babcock—there will be *no* more talk of zombies, or Grandma, or the... what was the other thing?"

"Trees," Mrs. Babcock said helpfully, climbing into the passenger seat of the car.

"Talking trees. For heaven's sake," Mr. Babcock said grimly. "You are *grounded*. You hear that?"

Norman slammed the back door of the car and, as an act of defiance, did not put on his seat belt.

"Grounded?" he asked incredulously. "For what? Being me? Because for your information, I did *not* ask to be born like this!"

"Yeah, well, we didn't ask for you to be born this way, either," Mr. Babcock muttered.

And really, Norman thought, hunched miserably in the backseat, *that's the problem right there.*

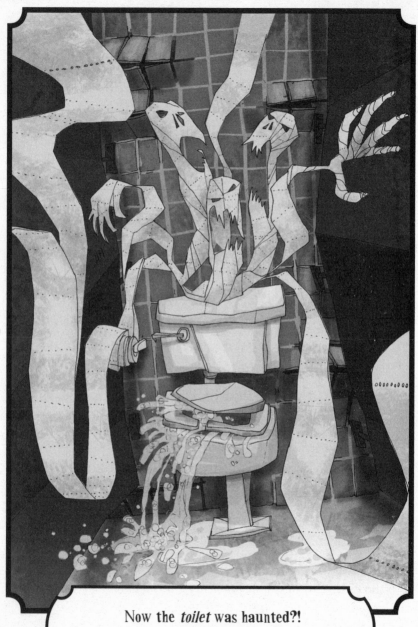

Now the *toilet* was haunted?!
What next?

Chapter Seven

Norman thought he had seen it all.

He thought he'd experienced his father at his most disappointed after the funeral. But the scathing lecture Norman received that night after the pageant put all previous Perry Babcock lectures to shame. Even Courtney gave Norman an earful, and she hadn't even been there, because she'd had cheerleading practice. And if Norman thought he'd seen just about the worst of the Blithe Hollow Middle School bullies, today was the day he was learning just how wrong he was. Maybe it was because he'd done it onstage in front of everyone, or maybe it was because it had something to do with the legend of the witch curse when the big anniversary was almost upon them, but the entire town seemed to be verging on hysterical about the whole subject, and toward Norman in particular.

Norman pulled open the door to the boys' bathroom, attempting to escape the loud and gleeful discussions of his "performance" at the pageant that were taking place up and down the main hallway of school.

Two of Alvin's Meaty Henchmen collided with Norman as they came out of the bathroom. One grabbed Norman by the ear, and the other put the death grip on his arm.

"Look, here he is now! So, did the tree tell ya anything else today, Norm?" asked the one holding his ear.

Meaty Henchman Number Two, a study in sports-related clothing and bad dental hygiene, laughed and squeezed Norman's arm tighter.

"Yeah, there's a bush outside the school—do you think you could ask it if the Yankees are going to win tonight?"

"Oh yeah, and, Babcock, can you let me know exactly what time the dead are coming? So I'm, like, not on the phone or something?" howled Meaty Henchman Number One.

Norman yanked his arm free and shoved his way into the bathroom, slamming the door in the Henchmen's faces.

"Morons," he muttered.

Norman sighed and leaned against the pale green

chipped ceramic wall, listening to one of the sink faucets dripping.

The sound of laughter erupted just outside the door, and Norman ducked into a stall and locked it. This was getting to be too much, even for him. He needed to be left alone, even if it was for just a couple of minutes. *I need to get myself together*, he thought.

The door to the bathroom opened, and someone came in. Without thinking, Norman perched on top of the tank, quietly closing the toilet lid and resting his feet on top of it. He held his breath, hoping his presence would go undetected. After a moment, Norman heard someone go into the stall closest to the door. He let out a tiny sigh of relief. Peace, if only for a moment.

But as it turned out, a moment of peace was all Norman was going to get.

As he sat atop the toilet, Norman's eyes fell on the industrial-sized roll of toilet paper attached to the wall. A scrap of toilet paper hung down and fluttered in the breeze.

Except there was no breeze.

Unable to take his eyes off it, Norman watched as the sheet of toilet paper bobbed gently up and down, then suddenly yanked forward violently, causing the entire roll to begin unspooling rapidly. Toilet paper shot everywhere like whipped cream streaming out of a can. What the heck was going on?

At that moment, the toilet on which Norman was perched began to shudder violently. Water began sloshing under the closed lid, spilling onto the floor. Norman yanked his feet away from the toilet, hunching in a terrified ball on the tank. He thought he might have heard a frightened squeak coming from the other stall, but bubbling water was spilling onto the floor, and it was making a lot of noise. Now the *toilet* was haunted?! What next? Whatever it was, Norman knew it was most definitely not good.

As he hung on to his perch, Norman watched with horror as the lid of the toilet began to slowly creak open. He squeezed his eyes closed for a moment, willing the whole scene to disappear. When he opened his eyes, he found that what he had hoped was a bad dream had just morphed into a full-scale nightmare.

Staring up at him from the toilet bowl was the greenish-yellow face of old Mr. Prenderghast.

Norman gasped in shock as an arm pushed out of the toilet bowl, followed by a second. As water spilled everywhere, the old man—or the ghost, to be more precise—hauled himself out of the toilet and stood ghoulish and dripping on the old tile floor.

"Yuh—you're dead," Norman whispered. "I saw you die in my dream."

"So what?" Prenderghast snapped. "I've got unfinished business here—the dead do sometimes, you know."

What the dead did *not* normally do was emerge from a toilet in the boys' room; normally they did not emerge from any sort of plumbing whatsoever.

"I know," Norman said in a small voice. "But this stall is already being used."

"You wouldn't listen to me while I was alive, so I gotta do what I gotta do now that I'm dead, and that means making you listen," Prenderghast hissed.

"I don't know what you mean," Norman said, pulling himself into an even smaller ball in an attempt to stop being dripped on.

"Because you never *listened* while I was alive!" the ghost yelled. "And that stupid family of yours forbade me to come within fifty feet of you! Look, I wasn't exactly thrilled when I realized it was *you*—that the last living member of this family who can speak to the dead was a Babcock. But someone's gotta take on my job, and that's you, punk, and I will haunt you from here to purgatory and back again until you *listen!*"

"Listen to what?" Norman whispered. "Do what job?"

Prenderghast scowled, toilet water beading in his transparent eyebrows.

"The job of stopping her every year," the ghost said.

"Stopping who?"

Prenderghast stomped his foot impatiently, spraying Norman's shoes with water.

"The witch!" he yelled. "How can someone with ears as big as yours be deaf? The witch rises each year on the anniversary of her execution, and she doesn't get up in a good mood. She starts getting good and riled up, and she summons every town member connected with her death and forces them to rise from their graves. Every year since it started happening, someone in this family who's got the gift of sight has to show up and put her back to sleep. For the last fifty years, that was me. You think I lived out by that graveyard just for kicks? And guess what, kid? Now it's your turn."

Norman stared at Prenderghast. In addition to looking like death, the old man really didn't smell very good, and coming through the toilet had not helped at all.

"But I don't know how—I'm only a kid," Norman protested, wrinkling his nose.

"It doesn't matter how old you are!" the ghost snapped. "The job comes to you, you do it. That's the way it's always been. You don't do it, she'll lay this entire town to waste!"

Norman was taken aback. The guy had just come out of a toilet, yeah. That got a person's attention. But all the same, this did not sound good. It did not sound good *at all*.

"Stop her how?" Norman asked.

"You must go to the place where the witch is buried and read from the book!"

Norman waited for an explanation but got none.

"Um, what book?" he asked.

Prenderghast made a loud, wet sound of irritation.

"The book in my hands!" he yelled, thrusting his two shriveled, bony, and very empty hands in front of Norman's face.

"Your hands are empty," Norman whispered.

"Not these hands, my *real* hands!" Prenderghast shouted. "The ones on my body."

"And your body is..." Norman suddenly remembered his dream. Oh geez. Was he supposed to believe that the old man's body was still lying where it had fallen in that dark room a couple of days earlier?

"In my house by the graveyard, on the study floor," Prenderghast said. "Not that anybody is going to think to look for me—nobody visits a crypt keeper. But you have to go there, Norman Babcock, and you have to get that book."

"Um, I'll definitely try," Norman said, wondering if there was any way to scoot around Prenderghast and escape from the flooding stall.

"Not just try—you *must!*" the ghost howled. "Before the sun sets tonight, or the witch will raise an army of the dead, and they will devour everything in their path! Swear it!"

In his frenzy, Prenderghast had turned upside down and was floating directly in front of Norman's head, a piece of toilet paper hanging off his ear.

"Okay, okay," Norman said. "I swear. But what do I do with the—"

The ghost of Norman's great-uncle Prenderghast immediately began to fade, bubbling and curling at the edges like an old photograph.

"My work here is done. Freedom!" Prenderghast exclaimed gleefully.

"Wait a minute!" shouted Norman. "You haven't told me what to do with the book—you haven't told me anything!"

The rippling image of the old man hung in the air momentarily, then burst into thousands of sparks of light, leaving only his fading cackle behind.

"You have got to be kidding me," Norman muttered.

After a moment, when nothing else crawled out of the toilet, Norman carefully climbed down, opened the stall door, and gingerly took a few steps outside. He noticed two things more or less at the same time.

The first was that the mirror over the little sink had cracked down the middle.

The second was that the occupant of the other stall was now standing in the center of the room, looking dazed and staring at the still-flooded toilet with his mouth hanging wide open.

"Oh, hi, Alvin," Norman said as Alvin continued to look at the toilet. "The, uh . . . guy before me did that."

Without giving Alvin time to recover—and he certainly would recover eventually and remember he had to beat up Norman—Norman slung his book bag over his shoulder and rushed out of the boys' room.

"Who crawled into your crypt and died?"
Grandma asked.

Chapter Eight

Norman paced his room, his mind racing. He had left school that morning right after the toilet-ghost incident by going to the nurse's office and pretending he had a throw-up bug. Given that he'd just seen his dead great-uncle Prenderghast come out of a bubbling toilet made faking not that much of a stretch.

Now it was early evening, and his parents had just gone out to dinner...and Norman felt as agitated and unsettled as he had since morning.

"Grandma Babcock? You around?" Norman called cautiously.

But there was no response.

"Great," Norman muttered. "Even the dead are avoiding me now."

What was he supposed to do with the information Prenderghast had given him? The ghost hadn't even stuck around long enough to explain what was in this so-called book, and how it was supposed to stop the witch from going postal on her three hundredth anniversary. And what was all that about an army of the dead? That was seriously warped.

Maybe my great-uncle Prenderghast just had a bizarre sense of humor, Norman thought, *and this was his idea of the ultimate parting joke?*

Something on Norman's desk began beeping, and he jumped and gave a little exclamation.

The beeping was coming from his cell phone. Norman walked over and picked it up, glancing at the text on his screen. COME TO THE WINDOW, it read.

Norman's heart started to beat a little harder, and his stomach tightened. Had Prenderghast switched from plumbing to cell phones now?

But when he walked to the window, he saw a single figure standing in his yard, his face obscured by a hockey mask, the eyes two sinister, blank black holes.

Norman's heart beat even faster. What was this? It was like that movie with the guy in the hockey mask—why couldn't he remember the name of it? He'd seen it, like, twenty times.

As his mind raced, the figure on the lawn reached a plump hand up, waved, then flipped the hockey mask off his face. Norman gave a great sigh of relief and shook his head.

Yanking open his window, he yelled, "Neil, what are you doing?"

"Did you get my text?" Neil called. "I stuck a note on your front door, too, just in case. I thought you might want to slap the hockey puck around or something. Or we could go play with Bub again!"

Norman sighed.

"Look, no offense, but I've kind of got more important stuff on my mind right now," Norman said.

"Is this about dead people?" Neil called.

Norman thought about just closing the window and ignoring Neil. Then he decided it might be better just to tell him the truth. He was acting kind of pesky, and the truth would scare him off once and for all.

"That graveyard guy we saw? My great-uncle Prenderghast? He died, and his ghost came out of the toilet to talk to me in the boys' room," Norman said, hoping his neighbors weren't out in their yards listening to all this.

Neil dropped the hockey mask on the grass and stared at Norman, his mouth hanging open a little.

"Whu—seriously?" he asked.

"Seriously," Norman told him, wondering why he wasn't already backing off the lawn to escape from the weirdness that was Norman Babcock.

"That doesn't sound very sanitary," Neil said. "I mean, he must have been violating, like, twenty health and safety codes."

"He's dead, Neil," Norman pointed out. "He doesn't care."

"Well, what'd he want?"

Norman hesitated. He'd gone with the truth so far—might as well stick with it.

"He said the witch's curse is real, and his job was to watch out for her and put her back to sleep every year on the anniversary. He said it's *my* job now, and if I didn't take some book to the old graveyard tonight before the sun sets, an army of the dead could rise and lay waste to our entire town."

Neil shifted from one foot to the other, his brow furrowed with concentration.

"Wow," he said. "That's epic, Norman. Are you sure you don't want to come play some hockey?"

Does irritable bowel syndrome make you stupid? Norman wondered.

"Didn't you hear what I just said?" Norman asked.

"Yeah, I heard you," Neil replied. "I just thought my idea was less likely to get us eaten than your idea."

Oh, great.

"Neil, there is no 'us' in this equation. I have to figure out what to do about all this myself. Just go home and rescue your brother, Mitch—he's probably trapped under his van again."

"But—"

"Go home, Neil," Norman called, slamming the window shut.

He turned to face the room and almost collided with something hovering directly behind him.

"Agh! Grandma!" Norman exclaimed.

His grandmother, wearing the same pink-and-blue tracksuit she wore every day, stared at him through eyes intensified by blue eye shadow. Norman could see his *Dawn of the Dead* poster clearly through her head, behind her pearl clip-on earrings.

"Geez, who rattled your chains?" Grandma Babcock asked.

Suddenly, Norman was tired of the whole thing— of the undead in general, and his creepy great-uncle Prenderghast in particular. He didn't want to talk about it anymore.

"No one," Norman mumbled, crossing to his bed and flopping down.

"Who crawled into your crypt and died?" Grandma asked, hovering in the air over the bed.

Down the hall, Norman could hear the sound of his sister singing in the bathroom, which she often did when she was applying makeup or attacking her hair with hair stuff. Things had been pretty tense in the house since the pageant fiasco, even with his sister. Norman dropped his voice a little.

"Dad says I'm not supposed to talk to you anymore," he said quietly.

"Poppycock," Grandma Babcock shot back. "The man's a blithering idiot. If I were a poltergeist, I'd spend my free time throwing stuff at his head. I've got enough problems of my own—the last thing I need is for you to stop talking to me. I'm supposed to be frolicking in paradise with your grandfather, you know. But I'm not."

This was something Norman had always wondered about. He sat up so his head was next to his grandmother's.

"So why did you decide to stay after you died?" he asked.

"Oh, I was never much for frolicking, to tell you the

truth," she told him. "And I bet there's no movie channels or canasta up there, either. Plus, I like it here just fine. I've got my hands full watching over you."

"Watching over me?" Norman asked.

"Sure. You know, making sure you're okay. Keeping up with the zombie movies. Checking in when your parents are being bozos. Whatever I can do. Everybody needs a little help sometimes."

Norman flopped back down on the bed, all the energy suddenly sucked out of him.

"You can say that again," he told his grandmother.

"Everybody needs a little help sometimes," she repeated. "And don't ever make the mistake of being afraid to ask for it. That's what your family and friends are for, and nothing's more important than that. Anyway, you're aces, kiddo. For what it's worth, I've got complete faith in you."

For some reason, Grandma Babcock's words made Norman feel better. He didn't have to be alone in all this—maybe it was better not to be.

"There's nothing wrong with being scared, Norman," she added, "so long as you don't let it change who you are."

He reached to grab his grandmother's hand, but she

was in the process of disappearing through a wall. As she drifted through it, she waved at him.

"Bye," Norman said to the wall in the otherwise empty room.

Then he sat on his bed, lost in thought.

Things had seemed easier when Grandma Babcock was still around. *Though I talk to her more now than I did when she was alive,* Norman thought. She was just a little old lady—no superpowers or anything. But she'd always seemed to make things a little easier. Just by being there.

Something made him think of Neil, standing in his front yard in that stupid hockey mask. Seemed like every time Norman turned around these days Neil was there.

And the thought no longer irritated him, not even a little.

"I can do this," he told himself.

Then he got up, grabbed his jacket, and walked out of his room. On his way downstairs, he passed Courtney, who was now wrapped in a fluffy pink bathrobe, her sparkly cell phone attached to her ear.

"So I said to her, 'Girl, talk to me when *your* basket toss gets twelve thousand hits on YouTube.' Yeah, no, I really said that. Oh, I totally can't. I'm stuck here on lame patrol—the night is going to be a total yawn."

Norman went around her, pulling on his jacket as he trotted down the stairs. She gave him a mildly disgusted look. *Why does his hair always stand straight up like that?* He looked like someone had hung him upside down to dry. This was America, the land of hair gel. Would it kill him to use some?

"Hey, what do you think you're doing?" Courtney called out. "No, sorry—I'm talking to my mental-case brother. He's doing something downstairs."

Norman pulled open the front door and stepped outside into the brisk autumn air.

"Norman, you better not be sneaking out, you little weirdo. If—"

The sound of Courtney's voice was cut off abruptly as Norman slammed the front door.

Norman stood on the front step, zipping up his coat. Then he took a deep breath and grabbed his bike from where he'd left it in the driveway.

"Okay," he said out loud. "Let's do this thing."

● ◆ ●

Now that he was resolved, Norman was determined to do what he had to do as quickly as possible. He rode his bike like a madman, pedaling as fast as he was physically able. As he shot over the bridge and onto Main Street, he took his eyes off the road for a moment to make sure he'd remembered to clip his cell phone to his belt. When he looked back up, he saw Alvin just feet in front of him, standing next to a boom box and doing some kind of ritual-looking dance while a couple of bored girls stood around. Norman swung wide to avoid the girls and swooped so close past Alvin that he accidentally clipped him. He heard an outraged *"Hey!"* followed by a crash that sounded like a thug falling onto a boom box, but Norman sped on without looking back. Norman Babcock had bigger fish to fry tonight than Alvin, with or without his Meaty Henchmen.

The dirt lane leading to Prenderghast's house zigzagged past a new development of houses surrounded by old evergreens. The sudden silence and lack of civilization was unnerving, as was the knowledge that at the end of this dirt lane was the old graveyard, and beyond that lay a vast tract of thick, old forest.

"Just get in and get out," Norman told himself, skidding to a stop in the dirt in front of an old, crooked mailbox that faintly read PRENDERGHAST on one side.

An ancient, mostly disintegrated metal flag was raised on the mailbox. *Does this guy get many letters?*

The house was an ancient, decrepit-looking structure of rotting wood. The old shingled roof dropped over the front of the house as if it had long since given up. The building seemed to be leaning off-kilter, and on both sides of the house, there were only two small windows, as if nobody outside would ever care to look in and nobody inside would bother to look out. It did not look like a happy place.

Norman leaned his bike against the mailbox and slowly climbed the steps to the path that led toward the front door of the house. He had ridden past this place a few times, but he'd never gotten this close. The little porch by the front door looked on the verge of collapsing. Everything about the house smelled of decay and neglect. The last thing in the world Norman Babcock wanted to do was go inside.

But he had to. He opened the front door and couldn't help hoping that this did not turn out to be, in fact, the last thing in the world he would do.

As soon as he stepped inside, it was pitch-black, as if the house had sucked every bit of light out of the world. Norman fumbled for his cell phone, his heart pounding. He pulled it from his belt and switched it on, the bluish light illuminating faded wallpaper and cracked floorboards. The house smelled of dust and something worse—food that had gone bad, or something that hadn't been washed in ten or twenty years.

"Hello?" Norman called. He instantly scolded himself. Norman had seen enough horror movies to know that when you walked into a creepy old house, you should never call "hello?" It pretty much guaranteed you were about to be chopped in two by an ax-wielding maniac.

The hall was full of junk—the cell phone light caught little slices of bizarre things. A shopping cart with a mannequin in it, a pile of broken typewriters, a huge bag that appeared to be filled with nothing but spoons. Norman carefully walked around a little mountain of doll parts, then froze as the light caught the outline of a teddy bear lying on the floor. For a moment the teddy bear seemed to be moving, but it must have been a trick of the light.

How did an old stuffed animal end up in a snake pit like this? Norman felt a little sad for the teddy bear, up until the moment he clearly saw one arm twitch, followed by a leg. Norman's heart was beating wildly, but he couldn't take his eyes off the bear, taking a step back as the head began to shake until it burst open and a swarm of moths streamed out. At the same time, the light on his cell phone flickered and went out.

Norman yelled and jumped backward, swatting his hands in the air and wincing as he felt little wings and bodies fluttering against his face in the dark.

Just move, he told himself. *Just find the room from the dream.*

As Norman's eyes got used to the dark, he noticed a faint stream of light at the end of the hallway. He moved carefully toward it, feeling his way along the wall, hoping there was a door there leading to the room he needed. When he got to the place where the chink of light was on the floor, his hands felt the smooth wood of a door and a cold round doorknob. Norman turned the knob and pushed the door open.

When he took a step into the room, he immediately knew that it was the one from his dream. Although the windows were covered with heavy curtains, enough light was coming in for him to see his surroundings in detail.

"What a dump," Norman muttered, looking around.

The room was an office or a study, and was crammed to the ceiling with all kinds of junk. Boxes were stacked haphazardly on top of one another. Newspapers littered the floor. In one corner, an old metal cot had been set up, and a dirty quilt and a stained pillow were piled on top of it.

"Did he, like, live in this room?" Norman wondered. "This guy really *was* nuts."

Norman took several tentative steps toward the center of the room, passing the desk he had seen in his dream. It was still covered with pictures of his family, and with pictures of Norman himself.

Creepy, Norman thought.

His foot hit an old rolled-up rug in the center of the room. As Norman started to step over it, he realized with a start that the thing on the floor was no rug.

It was the mortal remains of his great-uncle Prenderghast.

Norman made a face, and forced himself to stand his ground. He was used to dealing with the dead, sure. But not their bodies!

Don't think about it, Norman told himself. *Just find the book and go.*

After he oozed out of the toilet, Prenderghast had said something about the book. *The book in my hands*, Norman recalled the ghost saying.

Steeling himself, Norman knelt down next to the corpse. His eyes were growing accustomed to the dim light, and he could see now that the two waxy-looking white hands were, in fact, clutching a book. Taking a deep breath, Norman grabbed the book and yanked.

Nothing happened.

Norman yanked again. But Prenderghast truly had the death grip on the book, and it wasn't budging. Norman pulled one way and then the other. Finally, he sat back and braced his feet against the body and pulled the book toward him with all his might. To his enormous relief, the book suddenly came free, and Norman crashed backward.

Leaping to his feet, Norman headed for the hallway at a full run, the book tucked under one arm.

He did not stop running until he reached his bike, which he jumped on and pedaled like crazy—anything to get away from that horrible house and the body inside it. Anything would be better than that. *Anything.*

At least, Norman hoped that was true. Because he was back on the little dirt road pedaling as fast as he could toward the gate at the end of it—and the old graveyard that lay beyond.

Another twig snapped, and Norman sensed
the presence of evil behind him.

Chapter Nine

Norman Babcock stood in the center of the graveyard, where ancient headstones poked out amid long grass and tangles of thorns. He felt like a bit of a fool.

"What am I supposed to do now?" he asked. "The old man went to a lot of trouble to get me to do this. Would it have killed him to give some specific directions?"

He sighed. Maybe it *had* killed him. Or maybe Prenderghast had just died of old age, or of meanness, or of whatever disease you might get living in a rotting old dump piled high with junk.

Norman walked to the corner of the graveyard that was still getting the last of the setting sun, where the grass and undergrowth were the thickest. As he tried to make his way to the wall so he could sit down, he bumped into something hard in the grass.

"Ow!" he complained, stopping to clear the tall grass away so he could see what he had walked into.

What Norman had accidentally found was an old wooden sign that had fallen over and was almost completely overgrown with brambles. He cleared them away, revealing an epitaph that had been carved into the wood.

Here lie buried the seven victims of the Blithe Hollow curse. May these souls find eventual peace and everlasting salvation.

"The grave of the judge and jurors!" Norman exclaimed. He looked around and realized he was surrounded by a circle of headstones with their names and birth and death dates all listed. There was a Judge Hopkins and six other people—must have been the jurors. "They all died on the same day," Norman muttered. "Tomorrow's date—that's the day the witch was executed. So the story is true. She did something to them, a curse or whatever. They condemned her to death, and she somehow managed to take them with her."

Norman's arms went prickly with goose bumps, and a shiver ran up his spine. In light of what he had learned, this did not seem to be the greatest place to be hanging out on the eve of the three hundredth anniversary. Whatever had happened here was bad. Very bad.

"Okay, what did he say? He said I had to go to the place the witch was buried and read from the book. Before the sun sets. Okay, I'm here, and the sun is still up for another few minutes. So fine. I'll read whatever magic words need to be said, and then I'll go home. Maybe grab a double chili Witchy Weiner on the way."

The shadows across the graveyard were growing longer, and the light was definitely fading. Norman opened the book to the first page and began to read loudly.

"Once upon a time, in a far-off land, there lived a king and queen in a magnificent castle...."

Norman paused, then flipped through the book.

"Wait, this can't be right." Norman went through page after page. It was all the same—they were all stories about princesses and dragons and magical kingdoms.

"Fairy tales? The whole book is *fairy tales*?" Norman's jaw dropped. *Where are the magic spells to undo the curse?* That old man had been even crazier than he'd thought. Why he had ever listened to him in the first place...

He heard a twig snap behind him, and he froze. Another twig snapped, and Norman sensed the presence of evil behind him. Something large and dangerous. Something bad. He clutched the book and remained absolutely still. Suddenly, he felt a hand on the back of his neck, a spectral, icy hand.

Wait. Not so much icy. More...meaty.

Norman spun around.

"Whatcha got there, Geekula?" asked Alvin. And before Norman had time to react, Alvin snatched the book from his hands.

"Give it back!" Norman yelled. Alvin's monkey grin spread across his face—his special smile for when he was torturing another life-form. He held the book high over his head.

"Make me!" Alvin sang. "Whatcha doin', Normie? Come to read some bedtime stories to the dead peoplez? Alvin can't wait to tell *every*one about this!"

"Cut it out!" Norman yelled. "We're not even in school. What's your problem? Why don't you just leave me alone?"

"*Me* leave *you* alone?" Alvin cried, doing a little dance around Norman while still holding the book aloft triumphantly. "You made Alvin miss out on a possible date with a possible girl who was possibly about to compliment my epically awesome krumping skills. You ran me down on your bike, man! So, no way, dude, I'm not leaving you alone. You have to pay!"

"Oh please," Norman muttered.

"Beg all you want—it won't help! You disrespected Alvin, and Alvin don't like it! Now you want to run home to your mommy, but Alvin's not gonna let ya!"

This is insane, Norman thought.

The sun was barely peeking above the horizon now. Everything he'd done to get this stupid book and carry out his great-uncle Prenderghast's last order was now in jeopardy because of some stupid meathead bully who referred to himself in the third person. Norman took a deep breath and launched himself at Alvin, hitting him square in the midsection.

Alvin was caught off guard and landed flat on his back. Norman slammed on top of him, struggling to rip the book from his hand.

"Get off me, freak!" Alvin squeaked.

But Norman clung to Alvin like some kind of crazed squirrel, and the larger boy could not shake him off.

"Give it!" Norman yelled.

"No!" Alvin screamed.

Alvin's voice was drowned out by a massive clap of thunder, and a brilliant flash of lightning lit up the scene in a strange blue-green light. Both boys looked up at the same time, and both yelled in surprise.

The clouds overhead were swirling crazily like a bubbling potion. It almost looked like a giant face was peering out of the clouds. There was another clap of thunder and a gust of wind, and the face changed slightly.

It was grinning at them.

"Uh-oh," Norman said. Because although he had never seen her before, although no real portrait of the witch of Blithe Hollow existed, Norman suddenly knew that the face in the clouds was real. The face in the clouds was *her*. The swirling vapor seemed to be descending right onto the graveyard. Fingers of mist were now creeping across the ground. The wind howled again, sounding eerily like a human scream.

"We need to get out of here!" Norman exclaimed.

"Tell Alvin something he doesn't already know!" yelled Alvin.

The boys got to their feet, but before they could take more than a few steps toward the old gate, the ground started to rumble. The headstones around them began to grind and shift. One toppled heavily to the ground, and another split right down the center.

"What's happening?" Alvin shouted.

"I don't know!" Norman shot back.

And that was what scared him. Norman had no idea what was going on.

But he knew it wasn't good.

A golden orb of light shot up from one of the graves, followed by another, and another. Suddenly, the air was full of the spectral balls of light. *Spirit orbs*, Norman thought. Ghosts that had not re-formed in their earthly images. The orbs hovered in the air for a moment. Then, like a massive swarm of bees, they took off in a single cloud, over the cemetery gate, disappearing into the woods.

Whatever was happening was so bad, it had just scared off all the ghosts from the graveyard.

A pillar of fog shot forward along the ground and then reared up in front of the boys, morphing into something that looked like a giant hand. Norman stumbled backward, pulling Alvin with him, just as the hand thing plunged into the earth, as if it were digging for buried treasure. Norman fell, and he threw one arm up in a useless effort to keep the hand away. But something else was happening now. The earth beneath Norman seemed to be rippling and shuddering. Norman looked behind him and saw a tombstone that had shattered to pieces. He was sitting directly over the remains of the grave, and something was moving through the soil. Another crack of thunder and lightning erupted, and in the flash of light, Norman saw something push through the earth and loom in the dying light. It was a human hand.

"No!" Norman yelled, jumping to his feet and stepping rapidly backward.

"What was that? What *was* that?" Alvin was yelling over and over again.

Norman knew they needed to get out of there fast. But in every direction, the earth was buckling, and graves were bulging and bursting open. There could be no doubt about what was happening here. The dead were rising from their graves. It was zombie time.

The witch's army of the dead, Norman thought. *That's what Prenderghast said. That's what I was supposed to prevent by reading from the book.*

Norman had failed, and the dead were rising.

"Dude, we need to *move*," barked Norman, grabbing Alvin by the arm.

Alvin screamed and dropped the book.

Norman caught it neatly before it hit the ground and yanked on Alvin's sleeve.

"Come on!" he yelled.

Norman pulled Alvin toward the gate, navigating around several gaping holes in the ground. Without warning, a robed figure lurched in front of them, tugging at a foot still immersed in the earth in front of a headstone that read JUDGE HOPKINS. Alvin screamed again as the ragged and rotting creature bared his skeleton grin and stared with lidless eyes beneath the remains of an ancient powdered wig.

Stop, Norman thought he heard the thing say.

"What did he just say?" Norman cried.

"He said, 'Ugggggghbleaaaaaahhhhummmmm!'" Alvin yelled.

The zombie thing loomed over Norman, hissing and reaching his bony fingers toward the book clutched under Norman's arm.

"Run!" Norman shouted, ducking around the zombie judge and sprinting toward the gate.

Alvin was running, pinwheeling his arms and shrieking like a cheerleader who found a spider in her locker. Norman vaulted over the cemetery gate and grabbed his bike from where it lay on the ground. He glanced back and saw Alvin clumsily pulling himself over the gate. Behind Alvin, Norman saw a glimpse of something that chilled his blood. A crowd of stumbling forms in ragged and rotting Pilgrim garb. Zombies getting their footing. And this was no movie. This was real. Soon these zombies would be on the move, and nothing would stop them, because they were already dead. Anybody who'd ever seen a zombie movie knew what they wanted—to murder the living. And Norman had seen every zombie movie ever made.

Alvin tumbled face-first over the gate and onto the leaves. As Norman flipped up the kickstand on his bike, Alvin began to crawl forward toward him.

"Don't leave me!" he shrieked.

Norman hopped onto his bike. He might have considered it for a half second or so—leaving Alvin there to have his brain eaten by zombies. He paused just long enough to absorb the look of helpless terror on Alvin's face.

Wish I had a camera, he thought. "Get on the back, then!" he yelled, and Alvin practically vaulted onto the bike. Norman had to slam both feet into the ground to keep them from tipping over.

Alvin was heavy—there was no question about that. But the howling and keening sounds coming from the cemetery were utterly bone-chilling, and Norman used muscles he didn't even know he had, pedaling like crazy and speeding down the road away from the graveyard as Alvin clung, squeaking with fright, to his back.

But Norman knew his burst of adrenaline could not last forever. If there was one thing he knew, it was zombies. They might not come fast, but they were coming. To fall into their clutches meant certain death. They were way too far from town to get help, and the sun was now gone and the sky was green-black.

We've got to get out of sight, Norman thought. *We've got to hide.*

And there was only one place on this long stretch of road they could do that.

Norman gritted his teeth and pedaled for his life, heading for the dark shape in the distance, the only safety they might find out this far.

Back to the Prenderghast house.

"He's okay, right?" Courtney called from the van. "Let's go—tell him we'll call him a cab or something."

Chapter Ten

Courtney had been yelling insults at her brother from her room for about an hour before she realized Norman had never actually responded. A brief investigation of the house confirmed that Norman was not there at all.

"Great," she muttered. "He really did sneak out. Why would you sneak out of a house when you have no friends and no life? So what, am I supposed to, like, track him down? Aren't there beefy guys in uniforms who do stuff like this for their job? Maybe I could get that big guy from TV...whatshisname..."

Courtney examined her reflection in the mirror. She applied some lip gloss, and after some serious thought, she grabbed the hair straightener, heated it up, and ran it through her hair before putting it back in its signature high ponytail. Boys loved a high ponytail. Making it bounce turned them into, like, robots. It was a scientific fact.

"Where do I even look for that moron?" she asked herself, turning in profile and pouting her lips slightly to test the shininess of the gloss. "The mall, maybe! I could start at that Italian shoe store by the Space Ice Cream stand."

She grabbed her cell phone, whipped her ponytail around a little just to get it warmed up, and opened the front door.

Neil's note was still hanging there.

Hi, Norman,

You are invited to come over and play hockey or toss the ball for Bub's front half.

Sincerely yours,
Neil Downe (the house on Broome Street
with the red dragon mailbox)

Courtney rolled her eyes.

"Neil Downe?" she said. "That ginger dumpling? Puhlease. And Broome Street is on the other side of town."

She wished she hadn't seen the note, because it made it a little harder to justify looking for Norman in the Italian shoe store by the Space Ice Cream stand. If Courtney had said it once, she'd said it a thousand times: Norman Babcock was the reason for all pain.

Since you never knew who you might run into, Courtney ran upstairs and changed into her cutest outfit: a pink tracksuit with white piping cropped super-high so her entire stomach, including her epically adorable belly-button ring, was on display. She completed the outfit with a brand-new pair of pink high-tops that rubbed her ankle in a bad way. Her feet already hurt, but that was a price she was willing to pay to look her cutest.

"He's dead," Courtney muttered, heading for the bridge. "I'm going to kill him myself." It was going to take her a good ten minutes to walk there, which was ten minutes too long.

There was an olive house on Broome Street with a dragon mailbox. The rest of the houses were all shades of fading gray. Courtney limped up the driveway to the front door, muttering to herself. Her ponytail had gone limp, she had licked most of her lip gloss off, and one or more of her toes felt like they were about to snap off. She hated walking. It was just so totally unnatural.

Courtney rang the doorbell, and when no one instantly appeared, she banged on the door. Then she opened the redundant mail slot and peered inside.

"I know you're in there! You're only making it worse—the slumber party's over, dorks!" Courtney bellowed.

The door suddenly opened, and Courtney found herself face-to-face with Perfection in a Towel.

"Sorry," said Perfection in a Towel. "I was in the shower. Can I help you with something?"

Courtney's mouth dropped open. The guy standing in the doorway was truly ripped, with huge biceps. He was a big guy with rust-colored hair cut short like a soldier's—he looked like a Navy Seal crossed with a surfer dude. The only detail that didn't fit was the shower cap with rubber duckies all over it that was perched on top of his head. Other than that, the guy was...flawless.

Oh yes, you certainly can help me with something, Courtney thought, cursing the momentary lapse of reasoning that had caused her to leave the house without her tube of lip gloss. She could so totally tell she needed a reapplication. She tried to cover with a giggle—a high, silly one—and made big, round eyes. Boys loved that stuff.

"Oh, gosh, I'm, like, *so* sorry to bother you this late

and all, but I, um...I was actually looking for Neil Downe. Do you happen to know where he lives?"

Because clearly he could not live here, not Ginger Dumpling—not in the same house as Perfection in a Towel. That would be some kind of crime against nature, or something.

"Well, yeah, he's my brother. He lives right here. He's watching a movie in the den—it's up way loud, so he probably didn't hear the door."

Courtney let loose another wild giggle, but it came out wrong—too low. It sounded closer to a burp.

"No way!" she exclaimed, partly to cover up the noise. "Our brothers are, like, best friends!"

And if this wasn't true, Courtney immediately decided it would be her life's mission to *make* it true.

"I'm Courtney," she added, nodding to emphasize that Courtney was in fact her name, and because it would make her hair bounce a little.

Perfection in a Towel blinked a few times, like he was trying to figure something out.

"Neil?" he yelled over his shoulder. "There's a girl here asking for you!"

"Woman," Courtney murmured, but Perfection in a Towel was not even looking at her.

Neil appeared in the hallway, looking disheveled and lumpy. He was as not-spectacular as Courtney had remembered. How could he possibly be related to the Adonis before her? Oh well, he was, so she'd better give it her all.

"Heeeeeey!" she greeted Neil, nodding wildly to emphasize her total enthusiasm. "So *great* to see you!"

"I'm sorry, what?" Neil said.

"Silly, you know *me*! I'm Norman's sister," Courtney sang. She did everything but reach over and ruffle his hair, which, sorry, she was just not willing to do, even to impress Perfection in a Towel. "I'm here for Norman."

"Oh, but he isn't—" Neil stopped himself midsentence by smacking one hand over his mouth.

"He isn't what?" Courtney asked. *Please tell me Norman is in this house,* Courtney prayed. It would be devastating to have to go chase her brother in some place where there was no Perfection in a Towel.

"I mean, I have no idea where he is," Neil said. His already flushed face grew even redder, and little beads of sweat popped out on his forehead.

Perfection in a Towel narrowed his eyes at his brother.

"Start talking," he commanded.

Neil sighed.

"Well, he isn't here, Mitch," Neil said. "But he did mention something about maybe needing to go do something in the old graveyard."

"What?" his brother snapped. "And you let him go? Dude, that is a bad place any day of the year—everybody knows that. But on the night before the three hundredth anniversary of the witch's trial? That's, like, slasher-movie-crazy behavior. Only a nut job would do that."

"Oh, Norman *is* a nut job," Courtney said. "Believe me. This is *nothing*."

"I wanted to go with him, but he wouldn't let me," Neil said, scrunching up his eyebrows with alarm. "Do you think he's in trouble? Should we go after him?"

Courtney had just opened her mouth to say "no way" when her eyes snapped back to Perfection in a Towel. More specifically, the towel itself. An idea began forming in her head. She rearranged her expression into fluffy-innocent-puppy-dog face.

"I will be sooo grounded if he dies," she said. "I've got to find him, but I'm scared. Would you help me? Please? Mitch?" she added, because boys liked it when you knew their names. Boys also liked it when you asked for help. Everybody knew that.

"Oh man," Mitch sighed. "I told you that kid was trouble, Neil."

"He *is* trouble," Courtney said. "And if something happens to him, I'm totally going to get blamed! I would owe you superhuge if you could help me out this one teeny-tiny time."

Mitch sighed and shot an irritated look at his brother, then said, "Whatever. I gotta put some clothes on first."

Courtney fixed her hair as soon as his back was turned. She had to look Beyond Adorable now that she was actually going somewhere with Perfection in a Towel! Granted, it was a cursed graveyard at night, and there were irritating little brothers involved, but still. The evening was turning out to be a lot more interesting than she'd imagined.

● ◆ ●

"Ow," Neil said when Courtney shoulder-checked him in the driveway as he was opening the front door of the car.

"Sorry, do you mind if I sit up here? I get carsick," Courtney said, climbing into the front seat of Mitch's van.

Neil sighed and got into the back. Mitch, now dressed in a T-shirt that looked ten sizes too small and baggy shorts, put the key in the ignition. Courtney yanked the rearview mirror to an angle where she could check her reflection.

"Please don't touch that," Mitch said. "I spent an entire summer restoring this thing."

"And it totally shows!" Courtney exclaimed. "So, anyway, like I was saying, she told me I could totally consider a career in synchronized swimming. But I was like, 'I wanna do something that helps people less fortunate than me.' You know—like people who don't have TV or access to basic hair-care equipment. It's, like, so scary! I'm really into the environment, too. We can't imagine what it's like in some parts of the world—there's a serious mall shortage! I want to help change all that because I'm a giver, you know?"

"Put your seat belt on," Mitch said as he backed the van out of the driveway.

Courtney didn't want to put her seat belt on, because it detracted from the pinkness of her outfit and went right across her exposed belly button, which was one of her best features. But you didn't argue with boys—everybody knew that.

"I'm totally for seat belts," Courtney said.

"It's the law that you have to wear them," Neil remarked. "So that just means you're for the law, which doesn't make any sense."

Courtney turned around and glared at Neil, then beamed a massive smile at Mitch.

"Do you use free weights? You are swimming in deltoids!"

Mitch blinked rapidly and cleared his throat.

"I've never used deltoids in my life, and I'm willing to take a test to prove it."

Courtney shrieked with laughter. "You're, like, *hilarious!*" she cried.

In the backseat, Neil rolled his eyes. *Kill me now*, he thought.

"Anyway, thanks sooo much for doing this, Mitch. I don't know what I'd do if something happened to my brother. He's, like...really special. I could have been at this amazing party tonight—I actually got invited to, like, three—but I wanted to stay home and spend time with him. Family is sooo important, and he's like a brother to me, you know?"

"He *is* your brother," Neil muttered.

Courtney whirled around and gave Neil the Death Eyes. The Death Eyes always used to work like a charm on Norman, shutting him up instantly, but recently he'd been ignoring them.

"Why are you making that face—do you feel like you're going to throw up?" Neil asked.

Mitch hit the brakes.

"Whoa. Nobody gets sick in my van," he said.

"Oh, Neil, you're so silly! Don't worry, Mitch. I never throw up," Courtney declared. "It's just not ladylike."

Mitch looked unconvinced, but he stepped on the gas again. Then his eyes grew huge.

"Whoa! What's up with the sky?"

The van was rounding a corner onto a wooded hill that led to the old chapel overlooking the graveyard. Mitch was staring openmouthed at a mass of seething thunderclouds in the sky, swirling and shifting into bizarre shapes.

Suddenly, Neil grabbed Mitch's shoulder.

"Look out!" he yelled.

Mitch slammed on the brakes and swerved just in time to miss two figures on a bike speeding down the road toward them. The van careened onto the shoulder and smacked past a tree. The side mirror of the van snapped off, and Courtney screamed.

"That looked like Norman!" Neil exclaimed.

The van came to a stop in a shallow trench, and for a moment there was silence punctuated only by the sound of Mitch smacking his forehead as he surveyed the damage to his beloved van.

"Um, you didn't hit them, which I'm sure you were worried about," Neil said.

"Do you have any idea how hard it is to get replacement parts for a van this old?" Mitch snapped. "I must have been crazy to come out here with you two. We're going home."

Mitch floored the gas and threw the stick into reverse to lurch the van out of the trench. He was trying to execute a U-turn, when suddenly another figure loomed up in the center of the road. Yelling, Mitch hit the brakes again. There was a sickening thud, like the sound of a frozen turkey falling off a high shelf onto a concrete floor.

"Okay, I think you *did* hit that guy," Neil whispered.

"Oh man," Mitch muttered, unbuckling his seat belt. "Are you guys okay?"

"I'm pretty sure I broke a nail," Courtney whimpered.

"Sounds life-threatening—maybe we should call 910," Mitch said.

"It's 911," Neil said. "And I don't think they come for stuff like that. Mitch...are you going to go out there and check?"

"No!" Courtney squealed. "It's dark out! It's weird here! Let's just go! We'll call 911 from your house!"

Mitch took a deep breath. It *was* looking pretty scary out there.

"Yeah," he told his brother. "Stay here. I'm going to check it out."

Mitch climbed out of the car and walked several feet down the road, which was illuminated by the van's headlights. The body of a man was lying by the side of the road, not moving.

"Uh-oh," Mitch mumbled. "Um...hello? Sir? Everything okay?"

Everything was clearly not okay—everything was getting less okay by the second. Not only was the man lying there like a corpse, but there were other things wrong with him. His clothing was ripped and tattered, and had a strange old-timey look to it, like the guys from the first Thanksgiving they studied in school.

There was also a smell. A bad smell. Like rotting cheese and bad meat. And was it the lights from the van, or was the dude's skin... green?!

"He's okay, right?" Courtney called from the van. "Let's go—tell him we'll call him a cab or something."

Mitch stood uncertainly, afraid to go any closer. Suddenly, the figure moved slightly and made a low groaning noise.

"He's okay!" shouted Mitch, relieved. "I think he just needs help getting up."

His nose slightly wrinkled, Mitch approached the man.

"Hey, buddy, let me give you a hand, okay?" he said.

The man did not respond, so Mitch leaned down, grabbed one of his hands, which was disturbingly cold and slimy, and powerfully pulled the man up. The man pitched forward, his head colliding with Mitch's chest. Then he slumped back onto the road. At least, most of him did. His body was back on the ground—legs, torso, and arms. But something was missing. And Mitch was clutching something between his hands.

Mitch closed his eyes for a moment, figuring he was a bit woozy from the stress of the accident. When he opened his eyes, he looked down at the thing in his hands.

And the thing looked back at him, staring at Mitch menacingly with only one eye, the other hidden in a withered, closed-up socket.

Then the one eye blinked.

"Ew!" Courtney screamed. "My hair!"

Chapter Eleven

At the moment Mitch was screaming and drop-kicking a zombie head into the woods, Alvin and Norman appeared on the road, racing back toward the van.

"Did you see that?" Mitch shouted. "That thing was just a head!"

"Just ahead of what?" Courtney called from the van. "So does he want us to call him a cab or not? Was he going to a soccer game or something?"

"That *was* his head, dude—I kicked it, like, a hundred yards!" Mitch cried. "A hundred yards is really far!"

"Uh, Mitch?" Neil said nervously. "I think he wants it back."

Mitch whirled around to see the headless body stagger to his feet.

"Guys, we have to get out of here!" Norman yelled as he approached them. "Start the car!"

"Norman?" Courtney called. "Where have you been? You are going to be so grounded!"

"Zombies!" Alvin screamed, clutching the back of Norman's shirt as they ran to the van. "Zombies! Zombies! Zombies!"

Then he threw open the door of the van and jumped in, hitting the floor with a thud.

Mitch was still standing, paralyzed, watching the headless figure flail around with his arms extended, feeling blindly for his head.

"This is not normal," he whispered.

"Mitch, come on! We've got to drive!" yelled Norman, climbing into the van behind Alvin.

"Wait, we don't have room for you two," Courtney said. "Why don't all three of you get out, and Mitch and I will go home and call all of you cabs."

The night was pierced by a chorus of yowls and groans that set Norman's teeth on edge. On the road beyond Mitch, he could see a group of zombies closing in on them, lurching unsteadily on their rotting feet.

"They found us!" Norman yelled. "Mitch, we have to get out of here!"

Mitch took one look at the small dead crowd shuffling his way and immediately saw the logic in Norman's suggestion. He sprinted to the van and jumped in, locking the door behind him.

"What is going on out there?" Mitch asked.

"Drive first, questions later," Norman said.

"Okay, that's kind of rude, because it is Mitch's van," Courtney pointed out, because everyone knew boys liked people to remember stuff like that.

But Mitch was already starting the car and gunning the engine. The tires squealed and the muffler belched exhaust as the van careened back onto the road and away from the approaching creatures.

"Okay, talk," Mitch said. "What were those things?"

"Zombies," Norman said.

"Oh please," Courtney snapped. "Norman, you are so immature! Mitch isn't going to fall for your stupid *Dawn of the Dead* crap."

Mitch gripped the wheel tightly. "That guy's head came off in my hands," he said. "And the head looked at me, and then the body got up by itself."

There was a silence.

"Okay, fine, so they're zombies," Courtney said. "What's the big deal—live and let live, right?"

"They're not alive, Courtney," Norman snapped. "That's what makes them zombies. They're the living *dead,* and they're after us. They almost got me and Alvin at the graveyard."

"Who?" Courtney asked, turning around in the seat to stare at Alvin for the first time.

Alvin stared back at Courtney, his eyes enormous. His hands got all sweaty, and the blood rushed to his face.

"I'm Calvin," he said. "I mean Kevin. I mean Albert. Uh..."

"That's Alvin," Norman said with a sigh.

"Awkward," Neil chimed in.

Alvin sat up straight and pulled himself together, his thug face momentarily restored. "Alvin, yeah," he said. "So listen, you don't need to worry about a thing, blondie. Alvin's here now. I fought those things off before—basically saved your brother's life, no biggie. I'll protect you."

"Ew. As if," Courtney said. Like this jarhead was any competition for Perfection in a Towel.

There was a thud from the back of the van, and Alvin shrieked and dove onto the floor by Norman's feet.

"Impressive," Norman muttered. "Look—I'm not exactly sure what's going on, but something's gone nuclear with the witch's curse. The sun went down, there were crazy lights in the sky, and suddenly all the graves were opening up and those things were clawing their way out. Now they're after us."

"This is so typical," Courtney said. "I knew this was going to happen. I knew it!"

"You did?" Mitch asked. "Wow. 'Cause that zombie bit really threw me. If you had mentioned it, I never would have agreed to help your brother out."

"Help me out?" Norman said. "Neil, I told you I needed to do this alone."

"Then what's Alvin doing with you?" Neil asked.

"I didn't invite him," Norman said. "You don't understand—this is something I need to do myself. It's not your problem."

"Doing it yourself doesn't seem to be working out so good," Neil pointed out. "And you're my friend—so it *is* my problem. And those zombie things are headed toward town, so, actually, this is about to be everybody's problem."

Norman was about to tell Neil that he didn't want or need any friends, but something stopped him. Maybe it was what Grandma Babcock had said, or maybe it was just the strange, comfortable feeling he got when Neil said he was his friend.

"Look, can you guys go be BFFs somewhere else?" Courtney asked. "Because I'd really like to get to know Mitch a little better, which I totally can't do with you dorks blabbing in the backseat like a bunch of monkeys on a sugar high, so let's just—"

Courtney was interrupted by a terrible ripping sound, like a giant can opener slicing into metal. Norman looked up in time to see a section of the van's roof being ripped away and the face of the dead judge from the graveyard peering down. A bony hand thrust blindly into the van, just inches from Courtney's head.

"Courtney!" Norman yelled. "Zombie attack!"

"That's a little overdramatic, don't you think?" Courtney asked. "That guy didn't—"

The judge's hand connected with Courtney's head, the clawing fingers closing around her ponytail.

"Ew!" Courtney screamed. "My hair! Zombie attack!"

Courtney swatted the hand away, but the judge's head and body were through the hole in the roof now. He reached out again, this time for Norman's neck.

"Get off my friend!" Neil yelled, grabbing the book from Norman's lap and smashing it on the bony wrist. "Mitch, what do we do?"

"How should I know?" yelled Mitch, struggling with one hand on the steering wheel, the other one smacking at the zombie.

"Well, you're the oldest," cried Neil, battering the book over and over again against the zombie's wrist.

"Not mentally!" protested Mitch, hitting the brakes, then the gas, then the brakes again.

"Norman, you know stuff about zombies," Courtney pleaded. "How do we get this thing out of here?"

Mitch spun the steering wheel, and the van careened to the left, temporarily sending the thing off balance. For the moment, the zombie disappeared from the hole in the roof. They heard scrabbling sounds as he struggled to keep his hold on the roof. Every few moments, Mitch executed a swerve to keep the thing from getting a good grip.

"I think it's after me," Norman said. "I've got this book—I was supposed to go and read from it in the graveyard—it was supposed to stop this from happening."

"It didn't work," Neil pointed out.

"I know that," Norman snapped. "I did what Prenderghast said. I don't know what else to do."

"Prenderghast?" Courtney exclaimed. "Great-Uncle

Crypt Keeper? Oh man, Dad is going to cream you if he finds out you talked to him."

"Okay, what exactly did he say to do?" Neil asked.

"He told me to take the book to the witch's grave and read out loud," Norman said.

"Well, maybe you were supposed to stand at the exact place she was buried," Neil suggested. "I mean, did you?"

Norman stared at Neil.

"I don't know," he said. "I don't know where the exact place is. How was I supposed to find it? Neil, think!"

Neil looked panicked. "I'm not good at thinking," he said. "It's not my fault. My allergies make my brain itch."

The word *brain* stuck out, and Norman got an idea. He grabbed at his belt and exclaimed with dismay when he realized his cell phone was gone. He must have lost it in the graveyard.

"Courtney, do you have your phone?" Norman asked.

"Duh. When do I ever *not* have my phone?" Courtney said.

"I need it," Norman told her.

"In your dreams!" she said. "It's got genuine imitation Swarovski crystals on it—you'll just get it all sticky!"

"Courtney, there is a zombie still on the roof of this car," Norman said. "Do you want it to grab your hair again?"

Courtney handed over the cell phone as Mitch pulled another zombie-tipping swerve on the steering wheel.

"Where am I supposed to be going?" Mitch asked.

"Just keep on this road," Norman said, dialing the phone. "Um, hello, Salma? It's Norman."

Norman couldn't hear anything. "Hello?" he repeated.

"I'm here," came Salma's voice, with more than a hint of irritation.

"I have to ask you something important," Norman said.

"Norman, I already told you I don't let anyone copy my notes," she said. "And if it's about the bio test, I've already studied for it, so I'm afraid you—"

"Salma, listen," Norman said. "We really need help."

Tell her about the zombies, Neil mouthed to him. Norman turned in the opposite direction.

"Something terrible is happening," Norman began.

There was a howl, and the face of the zombie judge loomed through the roof. Alvin began screaming as the thing reached into the van and grabbed Courtney's ponytail again.

"I told you *not* to touch my *hair*!" Courtney shrieked. She fastened her hands around the filthy sleeve attached to the hand and yanked. There was a nauseating popping noise, and the arm came off in her hand.

"Gross!" Alvin squealed.

"Come on, man, be careful of the upholstery," Mitch wailed. "It's vintage!"

Courtney rolled down the window and threw the arm out. At the same time, Mitch hit the brakes, and the rest of the judge went flying off the roof and into the road. He didn't get up right away, and the van kept flying down the road, leaving him behind.

"What is going on?" Salma asked. "Norman, you aren't at a high school party, are you?"

"I don't have time to explain," Norman said. "I need to find the witch's grave—I need to find it tonight."

"The witch's grave? The Blithe Hollow Witch?" Salma asked.

"I couldn't find a headstone in the cemetery," Norman said.

"Well, of course not," Salma said. "First of all, I have to correct you in your use of the word *witch*. From a historical perspective, it's clear that this person was simply the victim of mass hysteria and a mob mentality taking the convenient guise of moral outrage and using the law as its personal thug squad meting out terror disguised as justice. At the very least, she should be called the *alleged* witch, which is something people in this town can't seem to—"

"Okay, I need to find the grave of the *alleged* witch!" Norman interrupted. "So, what, did they bury her without a headstone?"

"She wouldn't be in the cemetery," Salma said, speaking slowly and patiently as if Norman were extra stupid. "Cemeteries are consecrated ground—the religious Pilgrims never would have buried an alleged witch there. No chance."

"Then how do I figure out where she was buried?" Norman burst out. "Salma, I have to find that grave—the fate of the entire town may depend on it."

"Well, yes, the site should be located and properly commemorated," Salma said. "This town has racked up enough bad karma for a lifetime. Look, I covered all this for my extra-credit project for Mrs. Henscher last year. The trial took place in the Town Hall, on Main Street—the original center section of it used to be the courthouse. They have a bunch of letters and documents stored in the Hall of Records, though why everybody seems so proud of the fact that a mob went nuts and went after some poor old woman is beyond me. We thought the Romans were bad having prisoners fight lions in the Colosseum, but this is—"

"Documents? What would I look for in the documents?" Norman asked.

Salma sighed.

"There are files for every court case," she said. "You can find out who was there when she was executed, and what they did afterward. I'm presuming that includes what they did with the body."

"Salma, you're the best! Thanks!" Norman said.

"But wait—what—?"

Norman snapped the phone shut.

"Mitch, head for Main Street," he said. "We've got to get to the Town Hall; it's our only hope!"

Mitch groaned. "You mean this isn't over?"

"Nowhere close," said Norman. "But at least we have a plan now. But we have to hurry. Can't this thing go any faster?"

Mitch glanced over his shoulder long enough to give Norman an outraged look.

"Of course it can!" he exclaimed. "This baby's got a six-cylinder engine—a classic V6 turbocharged! Sweetest motor on the face of the planet! This thing is legend, man!"

"So . . . we can go faster?" Norman reminded him.

Mitch floored it. Neil and Norman grabbed on to each other, and Alvin slid off his seat face-first and tumbled downward, his feet sticking in the air.

"Nice," Courtney said.

"Um, Mitch," Neil said nervously, looking behind him. "I see flashing lights. I think it's the police."

"Oh great," Mitch said. "Do you have any idea what a speeding ticket will do to my insurance premium?"

"Forget them for now," Norman urged. "Keep driving. They can only give you one speeding ticket. Get us to the Town Hall!"

A police cruiser pulled up close behind the van, blaring its siren and flashing its lights.

"Great," Mitch muttered. "This night can officially not get any worse."

Courtney's cell phone rang—a distressing ringtone of a hip-hop version of "I Feel Pretty"—and Norman answered it.

"Norman? It's Salma. I don't know if this has anything to do with what you were just asking about, but
I'm looking out the window, and there's some pretty
weird stuff going on in town."

"Weird like how?" Norman asked.

"First, Mrs. Henscher just ran by in her bathrobe
with one of those green face masks, screaming. And I
just got a look at what she was running from."

"What?" Norman asked.

"They came out of the woods," Salma said. "It flies
in the face of most accepted medical research and
doesn't fit with the viability of the biological form after
organ failure and decay, but I know what I saw, and
there's lots of them, and they're all over town."

"What did you see?" Norman asked quietly.

"They're heading for the town square, and they
don't look happy."

"What did you see, Salma?" Norman asked again,
though he already had a pretty good idea what she saw.

Salma sighed, and when she spoke, her voice sounded
tiny and strange through the phone.

"Zombies," Salma said. "I saw zombies."

Mitch is wrong, Norman thought. The night had
officially just gotten worse.

At first, no one seemed to notice the zombies
shuffling into their midst.

Chapter Twelve

Five pairs of eyes silently scanned the sidewalks as Mitch turned the van onto Main Street.

"Looks pretty quiet," Neil said.

"I knew it," Courtney said. "Guys, we have totally been punked. This is, like, a senior prank or something."

"I hear something," Alvin said. "What is that?"

Everyone listened intently.

"It sounds like a pack of coyotes," Neil said.

"No, it sounds more like the tornado warning siren," Norman said.

"You're both wrong—it sounds like the saxophone section of the middle school band," Courtney said.

All three of those were pretty alarming noises—especially the last one. The group sat in silence, nervously looking around.

"It's getting louder," Norman said. "It's coming from right ahead of us."

That was when they saw it—and it was one of the scariest things they'd seen all night.

It was Mrs. Henscher. She was running down the street at full speed, waving her arms wildly as if she were being attacked by legions of phantom bats. Her powerful voice was keening a high-pitched banshee shriek. When she caught sight of the van, she bellowed out a warning without slowing down.

"By the pricking of my thumbs, *something wicked this way comes!*"

Then she rushed past and continued down Main Street, resuming her wordless howling.

"That can't be good," Neil observed.

"What in the world could make Mrs. Henscher run that fast?" wondered Alvin.

Neil and Norman exchanged a look.

"Zombies!" they exclaimed in unison.

"Mitch, drive!" Norman yelled.

Mitch hit the gas, and the van careened forward. They zoomed onto the street and quickly came up on Mrs. Henscher, who was still running smack in the middle of the road.

"Look out!" shrieked Courtney.

Mitch threw the wheel to the right, and the van

missed Mrs. Henscher by inches, then continued over a sidewalk and through an empty parking lot, and slammed into an enormous billboard with a drawing of the Blithe Hollow Witch holding a carton of french fries and huge letters proclaiming 300 YEARS! RELIVE THE HORROR AND GRAB A SNACK AT WITCHY WEINER!

There was a brief silence, interrupted by the sound of a hubcap falling onto the pavement. Wordlessly, everyone got out of the van and surveyed the damage.

"I'm gonna be sick," Mitch groaned.

"I think I broke a nail!" Courtney exclaimed, holding her hand up in the air to examine it.

"I think I broke a leg," Alvin moaned, disproving his theory by hopping around the parking lot in mock pain.

"We're okay, right?" Neil asked Norman.

Norman nodded grimly, looking around. It was too silent—the kind of quiet you hear just before something very loud happens.

"I'm so sorry, baby," Mitch murmured. "My poor girl, the last thing in the world I wanted was for you to get hurt. We're gonna get through this together."

Courtney hiked up her ponytail and adjusted her shirt and prepared to tell Mitch in a halting and clearly traumatized voice that she intended to forgive him. Then she realized he was speaking to his van.

"She's gonna take all winter to refit," Mitch said gloomily.

"Well, I actually feel responsible," Courtney said, not ready to give up on Perfection in a Towel. "So maybe I can help you. I don't know anything about cars, but I could get you sodas and rub your shoulders. Deal?"

"On the bright side, if we're all hacked to pieces by zombies, you're not going to have to worry about refitting your van," Norman said. "Guys, we need to *go*."

"Yeah," Neil added. "We should still have time to beat them to the Town Hall, unless they take the shortcut through the alley. But they couldn't possibly know about that."

"Perfect," Courtney said. "Mitch is crying over his personal vehicle, and now the geeks are in charge? Like, who's supposed to protect *me*? I mean, I've seen zombie movies, too, and everybody knows the cutest girl is always the first to die."

"I'll protect you," declared Alvin, stepping in front of Courtney and puffing himself up in an imitation of Mitch's bodybuilder form.

"Oh, that makes me feel *so* much better," Courtney

said. "So far, I've seen you scream like a girl and hide on the floor. No zombie army can stand up to that kind of defense."

"Yeah!" Alvin agreed. Then his eyebrows creased slightly as he replayed Courtney's comment in his head and tried to figure out if it really was a compliment.

Norman suddenly had a terrible thought. The zombies were heading for the center of town. It was a Friday night, and the partying leading up to tomorrow's anniversary gala would already be gearing up. There were going to be people outside, everywhere. Sitting ducks.

"We've got to warn everybody!" Norman shouted suddenly. And he took off in a sprint down Main Street toward the town square.

Neil was shouting something behind him about going too fast, but Norman didn't slow down. He ran until his lungs were about to burst, stopping only when he reached the border of the square. As he feared, it was filled with people.

"Hey!" Norman yelled, but there was too much activity going on, and no one seemed to hear him.

At that same moment, some newcomers appeared from an alley and stood surveying the square. Norman's blood ran cold.

The undead had arrived.

At first, no one seemed to notice the zombies shuffling into their midst. There was a group of people sitting at a picnic table outside the Witch Café, focused intently on an enormous bucket of fried chicken and Tater Tots. A loud woman in an oversize trucker cap was arguing over a drumstick with a young girl in a pink T-shirt that proclaimed DA RULEZ DON'T APPLY 2 ME. As they bickered with each other and clung to the drumstick, Norman watched in horror as a zombie shuffled over to them and stood there swaying, one eyeball dangling from its socket.

"Hey!" Norman yelled again, but this time his voice came out as little more than a croak.

One door down, outside Blithe's Quality Market, a group of high schoolers were smashing stolen shopping carts into one another. Another was whacking a lacrosse stick against a parking meter in an attempt to bust it open. A skinny, stooped zombie staggered toward them. As he moved, Norman could see that the back of his head had popped open, and brain matter was oozing out.

Norman heard wheezing gasps coming from directly behind him, and he whirled around, fists raised.

"Dude, it's only us!" Neil said, his face bright red and his body quivering as he panted like a racehorse.

"I think I tore a ligament in my leg," Courtney said. "Or I broke something—what do you call that thing you need for walking?"

"Your Abilities Tendon," Mitch told her.

"Oh, that sounds bad. Mitch, do you think you can carry me?"

Mitch was the only one not out of breath. However, he showed no signs of being willing to pick up Courtney.

"Do you see what we see?" Neil asked his brother, pointing at a zombie with maggots wriggling out of his ears standing outside TV World, transfixed by his own image. An oblivious woman in stiletto boots, leather jeans, and a fur-lined vest walked by them while chatting on a cell phone.

"I paid twenty-five thousand dollars for that purse," she was saying. "It's albino python skin and solid gold hardware. Gotta use your credit cards or they'll take 'em away, right?"

There was a moist-sounding thud as the stiletto-boot woman collided with something. It was another zombie, a short, squat figure with black-green skin, his head surrounded by a cloud of buzzing flies.

"Hey, watch where you're going!" snapped the woman. "This outfit cost more than you make in a—"

There was a moment of silence, and it seemed like everything in Blithe Hollow, living and dead, had paused. Then the woman dropped her phone, opened her mouth, and screamed at the top of her lungs. Over at the Witch Café, the woman and the girl dropped the drumstick and hurled the fried chicken bucket at the loopy-eyed zombie as they screeched like freaked-out chimpanzees. At Blithe's Quality Market, the high schoolers had caught sight of Leaking Brain Zombie. One of them took a swing with his lacrosse stick and managed to clip his head. When a green-gray stream of soupy brain matter flew out of the thing's skull, the teenagers abandoned their shopping carts and raced into the street, shrieking and squealing. Soon, every man, woman, and child in the town square was scream-ing with fright. People were knocking one another down trying to run away, but the zombies seemed to be closing in from every direction.

"Looks like a pretty regular Friday night," Mitch observed.

"We're too late—they're everywhere!" Norman

yelled. "Let's get to the Town Hall. Our only advantage is we can outrun them."

"Speak for yourself," moaned Neil.

Norman saw a portion of sidewalk near the Bar Gento that was zombie-free, and he headed for it, gesturing for the others to follow him. But suddenly the door of the bar flew open, and Crystal, the owner, a woman the size of an NFL quarterback, barreled through with a shotgun in her hands.

"Somebody, do something!" the stiletto-boot lady screamed.

Crystal raised her shotgun, aimed it at a robed zombie in the center of the square, and bellowed, "Kill 'em in the head!"

Norman watched in disbelief as the crowd grabbed makeshift weapons—a cane, a rock, a crowbar. Someone came running out of the hardware store with an armload of pitchforks and sledgehammers, which people climbed over one another to grab.

"Seriously?" Norman said. "You can't kill them—they're already dead!" he shouted.

He regretted shouting instantly, as he had called attention to himself. In the center of the town square, near the statue of the witch, a cadaverous robed figure turned to stare at Norman with lidless eyes.

The dead judge.

"Run for your lives!" Norman yelled, taking off toward the Town Hall.

The night was full of the sounds of smashes and shatters as people swung their weapons and hurled bottles. Norman took a quick look over his shoulder and saw the judge stumbling forward, his mouth hanging open as if he could not believe what the once young and hopeful town of Blithe Hollow had become.

The crowd had temporarily gotten the better of the zombies, who were staggering away from the assault, their rotting hands held out in protection of their decaying faces. Then Norman heard the deafening sound of a gunshot, and he looked back again to see the judge teetering but still upright, a grapefruit-sized hole still smoking in his torso. The judge threw back his head and made a high yowl, which seemed to summon the rest of the zombies. As the judge retreated from Main Street toward the shadowed alley behind the Town Hall, the rest of the undead tottered after him.

"Now's our chance," Norman said. He raced down the sidewalk toward the steps in front of the Town Hall,

knowing by the sounds of Neil's wheezing and Courtney's squealing that they were following his lead.

The Town Hall looked even more out of place
tonight than usual, the three-hundred-year-old timber
structure sticking out like a sore thumb next to the ugly
modern storefronts of yellow brick and glass. Norman
ran up the steps and yanked on the heavy wooden door.
It was locked.

"Anyone know how to pick a lock?" Norman asked
the group.

Mitch, Courtney, Neil, and Alvin stood at the bottom of the steps and stared up at him blankly.

Finally, Courtney sighed impatiently.

"What about him?" she said, pointing at Alvin.
"He looks like a criminal. Are you gonna tell me a guy
with a neck that thick can't pick a stupid lock?"

Alvin's face brightened.

"Can Alvin pick a lock?" he exclaimed. "Sure, picking locks is ma thang. Watch and learn, dudes. Oh, and
hot chick," he added to Courtney, who perked up at
being called a hot chick.

"Uh, you better hurry," Mitch said nervously. "The
law just pulled up."

Sure enough, the sheriff's scooter had just pulled

up over by the Bar Gento. In a handicapped spot, of course, but apparently the police were allowed to do that. Sheriff Hooper hopped off the scooter. She was wearing the same uniform she'd been issued five years ago, before the doughnut shop had opened right next to the police station. Now every button strained, and as she strode toward the gun-toting Crystal, it looked like there were two puppies in the back of her pants fighting to get out.

"There are so many things wrong with that outfit, I don't even know where to start," Courtney murmured.

"Alvin, come on," Norman said. "Can you get us in or not?"

"Have no fear, Alvin is here," he said. "They don't call me the Phantom Prowler for nothing."

"They don't call you the Phantom Prowler at all," Neil pointed out.

Alvin stared at the lock, then looked around on the ground. Picking up a large rock, he hurled it through a small window next to the door, reached his arm through, and unlocked the door from the inside.

"What'd I tell ya?" Alvin announced triumphantly. "Alvin got mad skillz, amirite?"

"We need to get out of sight," Norman said. "Everybody, follow me, and pull that door closed behind us."

Mitch was the last one in, and when he closed the door, they were surrounded by darkness, with a slight amber light coming from the EXIT signs.

"Now what?" asked Neil.

Norman paused because he wasn't sure. Suddenly, the hallway was illuminated by a flash of brilliant white-blue light, and almost instantly, a deafening clap of thunder exploded around them.

"Artillery!" cried Alvin. "Alvin surrenders!"

"That sounded like it was right on top of us," Neil said, rubbing his ears.

"It was," Norman said.

"Norm, don't take this the wrong way, okay?" Neil said carefully. "But it seems like all this stuff—the crazy dead guy, the zombies, the bizarre weather—all kind of seems to be centered on you."

Norman took a deep breath. They were all staring at him, Mitch standing slightly behind Neil, Courtney tapping her foot impatiently with her hands on her hips, and Alvin hiding behind a huge ornamental plant decorating the hallway.

"Neil's right," Norman said. "I haven't quite figured it out yet, but it has something to do with this book I took from Prenderghast's house, and with the fact that I can talk to the dead. The judge and his zombies are after me, and the witch making this storm is after me, too. I'm the only one who can stop this, and to be honest, I don't know if I can. What I do know is that it isn't safe to be around me. You should all go—get out while you can. Go home. The zombies won't follow you there. They're coming *here*.

"They're coming for *me*."

Somewhere in this room lay the secret
of the witch's grave.

Chapter Thirteen

"Well, if you insist, I guess we'll all be going, then—" Alvin began, but he shut his mouth when Courtney slapped at the plant he was hiding behind, and large plastic leaves rained down all around him.

"Shut up," Courtney said. "You'd run away from a pygmy ant. I speak for myself."

"Well, you guys can do what you want, but Norman's my friend," stated Neil, crossing his arms over his chest. "If he's staying here, I'm staying with him."

"Well, he's my brother," Courtney said. "And I could probably get sent to jail if something happens to him, and do you realize that in jail you have to wear the same thing, like, every day? So I'm staying here, too."

"Well, Neil is *my* brother," said Mitch. "And I'm not gonna leave him alone with some crazy ghost whisperer being chased by zombies and witch storms."

"I'm not crazy, Mitch, and I'm not your responsibility, Courtney," Norman snapped. "I can do this myself. Go away."

Norman walked down the hall, looking for the door marked HALL OF RECORDS.

He should be used to it by now—being called crazy. Being the one nobody wanted to be around unless they had to. Somewhere along that wild van ride Norman had started to feel like they were working together—that they were a team, almost. Team Kids against Team Zombies. But no, that was stupid. None of them wanted to be here, except maybe Neil, and he was probably just being polite.

In the dark, Norman almost walked into an open door. Stepping back a bit, he could see lettering in the dim light.

"Hall of Records, this is it," he said.

Neil came up behind him. "Hey, guys, we found it!" Neil yelled.

Norman wanted to point out that "we" had not found anything. But now that he was in the right room, he had to move fast. Somewhere in this room lay the secret of the witch's grave. The problem was, the room was huge. One end was made up of ceiling-high glass windows, and the streetlights outside shone onto stacks and stacks of bookshelves and file cabinets.

"Woo," Courtney said from the doorway. "How are we supposed to find anything in here?"

"Maybe there's a librarian on duty we could ask," Mitch said hopefully.

"We broke in, remember?" Neil said. "Usually librarians don't work in buildings at night with all the lights off."

"Oh," said Mitch. "Well, that was all I had."

"Too bad," said Alvin, who had also come in through the doorway. He had a plastic leaf stuck to the front of his shirt. "Oh well. We should probably take off, then."

From somewhere in the building, there came the sound of breaking glass, and something pounding on a door.

"Norman," Courtney said nervously, "that doesn't sound good."

For perhaps the first time in his life, Norman thought his sister had made a very good point. Suddenly, he had an idea.

"Give me your phone again, quick," Norman said.

More pounding erupted from downstairs. Courtney hastily handed the phone to Norman without so much as an eye roll of complaint.

"Hey, Salma? It's me again. We're in the Town Hall."

"Norman, it's getting pretty crazy out there," Salma said. "I'm over at the police station, which is completely deserted, by the way, which I'm sure must violate several basic statutes because part of the taxpayer/law enforcement covenant sets forth—"

"You should stay home," Norman said. "It isn't safe."

"I'm on the second floor, near the drunk tank," Salma said. "I have a perfect view of the whole square and the Town Hall. I can see about six laws being violated right now—nobody in their right mind is going to come *into* the police station tonight. Oh, and listen, I'm pretty sure I saw your parents out there."

Norman hesitated a moment to absorb that fact. His parents, somewhere in the crowd. But he simply could not worry about that right now.

"Okay," Norman said. "I'm in the Hall of Records, but it's huge. I have no idea where to start looking."

"Do you have any help?" she asked.

Norman looked around. Neil was lying on the floor, catching his breath. Courtney was brushing her hair.

Mitch was scaling one of the stacks like it was a ladder. And Alvin had partially climbed into another plastic plant.

"Not really," Norman said.

"Okay, well, the really old documents are kept in special boxes that are waterproof and airtight. They won't be with the regular books or files. Look around and see if you can find any boxes like that."

Norman heard a deep yelp followed by several loud thuds as Mitch fell off the stack he'd been climbing and hit the floor, followed by several boxes.

"Dude, these things almost killed me! What are they made of? Like, steel?" Mitch groaned.

"Hang on," Norman said. "I might have just found some."

Norman put the phone on the floor, pushed Mitch's leg out of the way, and popped the box open.

"Well? What do you see?" Norman could hear Salma's tiny voice coming from the cell phone.

"Norman, just hit the round button and put her on speaker," Courtney said. "Mitch, are you hurt? I can totally give first aid. I've seen every episode of *Malibu Nurse*, and that's, like, a reality show!"

Norman hit the speakerphone button.

"There are tons of smaller files and folders in here," he said. "It would take hours to go through them."

"There should be an index card inside with a list of everything in the box," Salma said. "Whoa! People are going crazy outside! They're waving around pitchforks and toilet plungers like they're light sabers. Wait, but where did the zombies go?"

"I found it," Norman said eagerly.

"Oh, okay. Do you see anything marked something like 'warrants, examinations, or indictments' that's dated in the seventeenth century?"

"Yes," Norman said excitedly. "It says D515-605."

"Okay, there should be a folder inside that matches those numbers. Norman, this is going to sound odd, but there is a massive thunderhead forming over the Town Hall. It's definitely a cumulonimbus cloud, and it looks like it's developing into a supercell, but the rest of the sky is clear. From a meteorological standpoint, I'd have to call this an anomaly at the very least."

"I've got the folder," Norman said, pulling it out. "It's full of smaller folders—each one has a name on it. Rebecca Haverstrom. Mary Black. Thomas Pellington."

"I swear, you would not believe what is going on out there," Salma said, her voice much higher and faster than usual. "The zombies seem to have taken off, but the people are still going crazy, smashing stuff and screaming. Mrs. Henscher is out there with that green stuff still all over her face, yelling at people. Sheriff Hooper is hiding in her scooter—people are starting to hit each other now."

"Salma! The file! Which file?"

"Look for one labeled Agatha Prenderghast."

Norman's hand froze.

"What?" he asked.

"P-R-E-N—"

"I know how to spell it," he said. "Salma, the witch who was executed three hundred years ago—her name is Agatha *Prenderghast*?"

"Yep," Salma said. "Nobody ever bothers with that fact, but the information is on record—I found it myself when I was doing my report."

It couldn't be a coincidence. It was a small town and an unusual name. Old Man Prenderghast was Norman's great-uncle, and the witch must be related to him.

Which means she's related to me, too, thought Norman.

There was a loud thud in the distance, like the sound of a heavy wooden door being kicked in.

"What was that?" cried Alvin.

"Sounded like somebody broke down the front door," Mitch answered.

"Salma, did you say none of the zombies are in the square anymore?" Neil asked.

"Yeah, they all just disappeared," Salma said. "Maybe they went into one of the buildings."

"Uh-oh," Neil said. "Uh, Norman?"

"I'm hurrying," Norman said, pulling old, yellowed parchment from Agatha Prenderghast's file.

"Guys, Mrs. Henscher is working the crowd into a frenzy," Salma said. "She's quoting Shakespeare—screaming stuff like 'Cry havoc and let slip the dogs of war.' And she's pointing to the Town Hall!"

"I found something!" Norman cried, holding a ripped piece of parchment in front of his face so he could read the faded words. "Whereas Agatha Prenderghast has been found guilty of performing certain detestable arts of witchcraft and sorcery feloniously and maliciously within the Township of Blithe Hollow, against the peace of our sovereign lord, and by the statute of the first of King James—"

"Skip ahead. There should be something about her sentence," Salma interrupted.

"Here it is," Norman said. He swallowed. Just looking at the words turned his blood to ice. "It says she shall be taken to Knob Hill and...and hung by the neck until dead...that her mortal remains should be interred there, and that no member of her family may ever be buried in the churchyard or any consecrated ground."

Yikes, thought Norman. *No wonder the witch was so mad.*

"Knob Hill—that's across the river out by the old forest trail," Salma said. "They used to call it that because of the strange old trees that grew there and had bumps and knobs on their trunks. One or two of the trees are still standing, but they've turned completely white."

"I know that place!" Norman cried. "That's where I've got to go."

"Norman, don't leave that building!" Salma said. "There's a whole crowd gathering right outside the front door. They are out of control!"

Norman could hear them now, shouting and bellowing. Over the mob, he heard the unmistakable sound of Mrs. Henscher crying, "Find 'em and rip 'em apart!"

"What's wrong with them?" Neil exclaimed. "It's like they've all lost their minds—if they find us, what if they accidentally think we're zombies and come after us, too?"

"What did the zombies even do to make everyone hate them so much?" Alvin said. "I mean, yeah, they're crusty, rotting dead dudes and all, but why gang up on them just because they're a little . . . different?"

"Interesting question, Alvin," Neil said. "Maybe you ought to give it a little thought."

Alvin punched Neil in the arm.

"They've turned into a mob," Norman said. "They're all riled up to attack the zombies no matter what. None of their brains are working anymore. They're just going to do what everyone else is doing."

"That's the lamest thing I've ever heard," Courtney said. "People should think for themselves!"

"There are, like, twenty files in this box with names of people who were put on trial for being witches," Norman said. "I doubt any of the people who accused them were thinking for themselves."

"Guys," hissed Mitch, who was standing in the doorway, peering down the hall. "Something just moved down there."

"Zombies!" Alvin squealed. Neil smacked him on the back of the head.

"Stop screaming," Neil whispered. "Do you want them to find us?"

Alvin shook his head, one hand over his own mouth, his eyes huge.

"Everybody, get away from the door," Norman whispered. "Let's go over there by the window. We can crouch down behind that table."

Norman headed for the window and glanced out, then froze, transfixed by what he saw.

Salma had not been exaggerating. A large mob of threatening townspeople had gathered at the front steps of the Town Hall. Mrs. Henscher was on the top step, shouting at them, pointing to the Town Hall, and shaking her fist. The crowd rippled and moved like a single creature—a predator flexing its muscles just before springing onto the back of its prey.

"They've gone crazy—totally crazy!" Norman said. He could see that not everyone was taking part in the mob. Sheriff Hooper was on the outskirts, trying to pull people away. Across the street, Norman could see the outline of Salma at the window in the police station. On the street below, Norman caught sight of a familiar station wagon, which two people were in the process of exiting.

"Oh...no," Norman muttered. Salma had been right when she said she thought she'd glimpsed his parents.

He wanted to scream a warning to his parents to stay away from the Town Hall, but they'd never hear him. At that moment, a brick came flying through the window, and an explosion of glass rained down around them.

"Once more unto the breach, dear friends! Once more!" Mrs. Henscher was hollering. "Or close the walls up with our English dead!"

Through shards of glass still clinging to the window frame, Norman saw Mrs. Henscher rush to the top step of the Town Hall. The mob surged forward.

"We've got to run for it!" Mitch shouted.

Neil looked around and spied a fire escape map on the wall. "Everyone, down the back staircase to the lobby!" he yelled. "There's a fire door that opens to the back alley. Go! Go! *Go!*"

"Wait, where's the book? I lost Prenderghast's book!" Norman cried, looking around wildly.

"You lost a book in a room full of books?" Alvin exclaimed. "Forget it; it's toast."

"I can't leave without it," Norman said, getting on

his hands and knees and feeling around on the floor for it.

"Norman, forget the stupid book!" Courtney shrieked. "For once in your worthless life, do what I say!"

Norman and Courtney stared at each other.

"Wait, I didn't mean—" Courtney began.

"Leave! Just go! I *never* asked for your help! You only came along because you thought you might get in trouble with Mom and Dad. You think I'm a freak—admit it. *Admit it!*"

Courtney swallowed nervously. "Well, I have used that word to describe you on a number of occasions, but it's not totally out of line for somebody who hangs out with people who *literally* have no lives!"

"Fine!" Norman said. "I'm not leaving until I find my book, and all of you are in my way—so get *out* of here!"

"Look," Courtney said to Mitch, "I had Mrs. Henscher for homeroom two years ago. I know she's all crazy right now, but I think she'll recognize me. I mean, who could mistake me for a zombie? The crowd will realize there are kids in the building. Then one of us can come back for Norman if it's safe."

"Good plan," said Mitch.

"Great. Bye, Norman, nice knowing ya," Alvin said, dashing out the door.

"Well, I'm staying with Norman," Neil declared.

"No, you're not," Mitch said firmly.

Neil opened his mouth to protest, but Mitch simply picked him up and threw him over his shoulder, as if Neil were nothing more than a large bag of dog food.

Moments later, Norman was alone in the Hall of Records. He sighed, looking around the room. In the corner, near where one of the big boxes had fallen, Norman caught sight of something brown and rectangular.

"Is that it?" he murmured, walking over to the box.

Kneeling down, he saw with relief that it was Prenderghast's book. He tucked it under his arm, and then stared at the contents of the open box.

"So many names," Norman said, flipping through the files. "Vandervoort—executed. Trilling—executed. Boyer—died in prison. What were they doing? Just accusing anyone they didn't like of being a witch? For no reason? Why would people do that to each other?"

There was a creak behind him, a sound not so much like an old floorboard as like an old . . . bone.

Norman whirled around.

"No!" he yelled, shoving the box toward the hideous, leering creature lurching toward him, its arms outstretched.

Then he saw a second zombie, teetering by the center stack, and beyond that, more coming through a dim, tall rectangle in the wall. There was a second door into the Hall of Records. The zombies had found it, and Norman was cornered.

"Help!" he yelled. "Somebody help me!"

But he knew there was no way the others would hear him. He scuttled into a corner as two of the zombies began to close in. He recognized one of them as Leaking Brain Zombie. The second one, who had one eyeball hanging down and bouncing around, reached out its skeletal hand.

There was nowhere to go. Norman smooshed himself against a bookshelf and looked up and saw a red plastic plaque on the wall that said ROOF ACCESS—KEEP CLEAR. Sure enough, there was a trapdoor in the ceiling. Norman grabbed a few books and whipped them at Hanging Eyeball Zombie, then scrambled up the bookshelf the way he'd seen Mitch do it. Moments later, he was at the top. He shoved the trapdoor, almost yelled with relief when it opened, and hoisted himself up and through it.

• ◆ •

"Burn them out!" screamed Mrs. Henscher from the Town Hall steps, waving a flaming torch in the air. A cheer of agreement rippled through the crowd.

"Burn them!" someone shouted.

"Set fire to the place!" howled another.

Mrs. Henscher whirled around and touched her torch to the remains of the front door, which was hanging off its hinges. Courtney reached the bottom of the stairs in the lobby first and raced to the doorway.

"Hey, cut that out!" she bellowed, running to the door and knocking the torch from Mrs. Henscher's hands. But it was too late. A tongue of flame was racing up the dry, old wood of the door. The frame of the building was little more than kindling, and the fire raced over the surface, growing more powerful by the second.

"Have you all lost your minds?" Courtney yelled at the crowd.

"Yeah!" Alvin shouted, appearing in the doorway

behind Mitch and Neil. "I don't know much, but I know vandalism when I see it, and this is going on your *permanent records!*"

"Get thee hence, children!" cried Mrs. Henscher. "We have come for the zombies and the necromancers and the dabblers of doom! There is evil in that building!"

"Listen to yourselves!" Courtney yelled. "Look at us—we're just kids. There is no evil in that building, but my brother is still in there and we've got to get—"

Courtney's words were drowned out by a collective gasp coming from the crowd. Someone pointed up, toward the roof of the building.

"There!" someone shouted.

"Look!" yelled a woman.

"He's summoning a demon!" shrieked a mousy-looking old man.

Courtney ran down the steps and turned to look up at whatever had set the crowd off.

Over the roof of the building a massive, spiral-shaped swirl of greenish-black cloud was rotating. In its center was a face contorted with rage and fury. And directly below the massive swirling face was Norman, standing on the roof, waving a book with one hand.

• 173 •

"He summons the witch!" yelled the bar owner, still carrying her shotgun. "He is the witch's master!"

"*Necromancer!*" called Mrs. Henscher.

"Norman?" called a woman with a familiar voice.

Courtney whirled around. On the sidewalk, some twenty feet away from the mob, stood Mr. and Mrs. Babcock. They were staring at the unfolding scene on the roof, both of them slack-jawed.

"Uh, Mom, Dad, I can explain!" Courtney called. "Everybody—I can explain!"

But in spite of the fact that she was most definitely the cutest girl in the entire mob, nobody was paying any attention to her at all. They were shaking their fists at the building. She had to get the others out of there now. Everyone was transfixed by what was happening on the roof, and no one saw Courtney dash back inside the building.

• ◆ •

Norman had seen the massive, jeering face in the swirling clouds as soon as he went through the trapdoor that opened onto the roof. It grew bigger and bigger, and Norman could hear the mob on the street growing progressively more hysterical. The end of her huge green hooked nose was practically in his face.

"Stop it!" Norman shouted. "Why are you scaring everybody?"

The witch responded by growing even larger and shaping the clouds to bare her teeth in a menacing jack-o'-lantern grin. Her teeth were blackened and cracked, and her face was lit with an eerie green light. The crowd began screaming louder.

"You horrible old witch!" Norman yelled, stamping his foot. "You've created a monster down there. Are you happy now? Is this what you want?"

Norman looked at the book under his arm. It seemed ridiculous. But it was what Prenderghast had told him to do, and this thing...this witch swirling over his head...she was a Prenderghast, too.

As he opened the cover, he heard pounding on the trapdoor. He jumped onto it, slid the bolt closed, then ran as far as he could from it, climbing a ladder that ran up the side of a chimney to get close to the witch. He raised the book.

"Hey, you—listen to this!" Norman shouted. The wind was blowing so hard, he could hardly hear himself, and the force of it threatened to rip the book from his hands. But he managed to open it and began to read.

"Once upon a time, in a far-off land, there lived a king and queen in a magnificent castle—"

"Necromancer!" Norman heard a woman scream from the crowd.

The face in the cloud began to cackle monstrously. Norman slammed the book shut in frustration, seeing the columns of black smoke rising from the building and snaking into the air.

"This is what he told me to do! Why won't you listen to me? Why are you doing this?" Norman cried.

The hideous face in the clouds turned inside out, and from its center, a tongue of lightning shot out toward Norman, knocking the book from his hands and sending him reeling backward onto the old timbers of the roof. The wood splintered under the impact, and Norman plunged through the roof into the building, and moments later, black smoke flecked with orange sparks surged through the hole his body had made.

Am I dead? Norman wondered.

Chapter Fourteen

When Norman opened his eyes, the fire was gone. In his hand where the book had been, he clutched a tiny fragment of leather spine, burned black around the edges.

He sat up slowly, rubbing his aching head. There had been a fire—he knew that. Now there was none. He had come through a door from a room full of books, but this room was bare.

Am I dead? Norman wondered.

The room was simple and plain, with wooden floors and walls. At one end of the room was a platform where four grim-looking men and two grim-looking women dressed in the black garb of Pilgrims stood behind a table. A crowd of onlookers had gathered, keeping a respectful distance from the table but filling the room.

Disoriented and feeling queasy from the smoke, Norman wondered if he'd somehow fallen into a rehearsal for another one of Mrs. Henscher's pageants. Then, with a sick feeling, he realized exactly what was going on.

"This is a trial," he murmured.

A door opened, and a tall, gaunt man in a white powdered wig and dark robes strode through the door.

Norman recognized him right away. He had stumbled on his grave. He had fought his zombie.

Judge Hopkins.

The judge stepped up onto the platform and glared at Norman with cold, humorless eyes.

He can see me? Norman thought, pulling his knees to his chest and willing himself to disappear.

Now every eye in the room was on Norman. He felt a deep, icy fear in the marrow of his bones, and he began to shake.

"You have been arraigned for the detestable arts of witchcraft and sorcery. You have feloniously and maliciously performed evil works against your fellow townspeople, witnessed by these good citizens who have gathered here to render their testimony...."

The men and women in the crowd nodded, whispering to one another and pointing at Norman with expressions of unpleasant triumph.

"No," whispered Norman. "I haven't done anything."

"You have, by the jury of these six peers empowered by our sovereign, King James, been found guilty of all the grievous crimes of which you are accused—" continued the judge.

"No, please! You're making a mistake...." Norman whispered. His voice would not come out any louder. He was shaking so hard, his teeth were rattling.

"—and it is passed on you, according to your grievous crimes, the punishment of death by hanging."

Norman turned in the opposite direction to avoid the hungry gaze of the crowd, and he drew back, aghast at the sight behind him.

It was a girl about his own age, with hair as dark as his own, her wrists and ankles in chains, and her eyes cast down. Why was there a child here in chains? Was she somehow related to the old woman the town thought was a witch?

"Agatha Prenderghast, you are hereby sentenced to death!"

"*No!*" screamed the girl, looking up, flashing brilliant blue eyes. "I haven't done anything wrong!"

Norman gasped in disbelief. This was the person being tried for witchcraft? This delicate little girl with bright blue eyes? Surely even these people could not be that monstrous.

Judge Hopkins drew himself up to his full, terrifying height and strode toward the girl.

"Do you deny, then, that you have claimed to speak with the dead?"

Norman could see Agatha's small pale face was smudged with dirt and streaked with tears. It was true, then—the Blithe Hollow Witch was just a wisp of a little girl. Norman felt sick to his stomach. *How could they?*

"I only spoke to them because they spoke to me!" she cried. "Leave me be!"

"You have defied our moral code, and you have risked the souls of every good man and woman in Blithe Hollow. For this, you will pay with your life!" declared the judge. "Seize her!"

"No, leave her alone! She didn't do anything! Don't touch her!" Norman shouted.

A burly man came forward and walked right *through* Norman. He grabbed the girl roughly by one arm.

"Leave me alone or I'll make you sorry!" the girl shouted. "I'll make you all sorry!"

The man began to drag the girl from the room, and the crowd pressed forward to follow. Norman tried to go after them but found himself staggering as if the floor was lurching beneath his feet. The room began to spin, and the figures of the girl and the crowd were hazed over with a veil of swirling black.

"I'm going to get you all!" the girl screamed. "You'll pay for this forever. *Forever!*"

The hot, painful sensation of smoke filled Norman's lungs, and his legs gave way. He hit the floor hard, his eyes closed. The room grew hotter, and the smell of smoke was overpowering. He felt something poke his arm, and he opened his eyes. The seven Pilgrims, those who had sat around the table and found Agatha Prenderghast guilty of witchcraft, surrounded him. But these were neither memories nor ghosts.

They were the dead among the living. Agatha had cursed them, and now they were like this, decaying and hideous, reeking of death and incapable of communicating anything but terror.

But Norman was not afraid of them anymore. He sat up.

"How could you?" he asked. "She was a child! She harmed no one—and you had her put to death! A child!"

Judge Hopkins pushed through the group and loomed over Norman.

"Fine!" Norman snapped. "I'm not scared of you anymore. You want to kill another child? Go ahead. Do it!"

The judge leaned close to Norman, who could not help but recoil from the terrible smell and the yellow-green flesh of his face.

"Heeeeeelp us...." the judge whispered.

Norman froze, confused, and dizzy from the smoke thickening the air.

"Help *you*?" he asked.

"She is angry," the judge said. "The others, they read to her from the book, until she slept."

The others. His great-uncle Prenderghast and his ancestors.

"Well, that isn't working anymore," Norman said. "She's not just angry anymore—she's in an out-of-control rage because of what you did to her. I don't know if anyone can stop her now. She may take all of Blithe Hollow with her this time."

The dead judge hung his head. The six other zombies shook their heads with despair, groaning.

"Why did you do it?" Norman asked.

"She scared us," the judge said. "She communed with those who were no longer living."

"So what?" Norman asked. "I'm doing that right now. I'm talking to you, and you're no longer living." As he said it, Norman realized it was true. Apparently, he could talk to more than just ghosts.

The judge managed to look ashamed.

"We didn't understand," he said. "She didn't behave like the rest of us. We thought her difference made her dangerous. We thought it made her powerful."

"It did," Norman said. "Look what she managed to do to you."

The judge wrung his bony hands.

"Help us," he pleaded. "Tell us what we can do."

Norman didn't think the judge and his fellow zombies deserved help. They had ganged up on someone who'd never done a thing to them and attacked her in the worst possible way. They were vintage bullies—they made Alvin and his Meaty Henchmen look like kittens.

But somehow the cycle had to stop. Not for the zombies' sake, but so that Agatha could find peace.

"I know you took her to Knob Hill," Norman said. "I need you to tell me exactly where you buried her. I need to go there and talk to her."

The zombies stared at one another nervously.

"Don't worry," Norman said, getting up and brushing the soot from his jeans. "I'm going to help you."

• ◆ •

In the smoke-filled lobby of the Town Hall, an ancient roof timber covered with flames plummeted to the floor with a crash.

"Under here! Quick!" Mitch shouted, dragging Courtney and Neil by their shirts toward the massive oak reception desk.

"There's room next to me for Courtney," Alvin squeaked, already curled up under the desk. He made another squeak when Neil, not Courtney, squished up against him.

"Mitch Downe, in spite of your heroic efforts to save us, we could, like, die tonight," Courtney said, grabbing his muscled arm. "This might be the last chance I have to talk about my feelings."

"Uh, unless we come back as zombies. Then, technically, you would have more time," Mitch pointed out.

"Well, maybe, but—"

"Someone's coming down the stairs!" Neil shouted.

"Zombies!" yelled Alvin, trying to pull Neil on top of him as a shield.

"Wait, I see Norman! They have Norman!" Courtney cried, scrambling out from under the desk. "What is he doing?"

Norman was walking in the center of the zombies, his mouth and nose covered by his sleeve to keep out the smoke. He was escorted by seven zombies in tattered black robes, lurching and tottering through the smoke to the door.

Another massive beam swung down from the ceiling like a pendulum, crashing in an explosion of sparks into the remains of the front door, which flew into pieces.

"Go, now! Go!" shouted Mitch.

The gang shot through the door and got out of the way, climbing to the side of the steps and blending into the front of the crowd as Norman and the zombies appeared, framed by orange light and billows of smoke.

A single noise of surprise came from the crowd, and they moved back several feet. Sheriff Hooper stepped forward, holding her gun in one trembling hand and gesturing at the zombies.

"You, there, stay where you are! I don't care how dead you all are—I will shoot if I have to!"

Norman pushed his way to the front of the zombies and held his hands out.

"No, you won't!" he cried.

The crowd looked even scarier up close than Norman had thought it would. But he stood his ground, making eye contact with as many people as possible, trying to remind them that they were all in this together.

"It's Norman!" came a high, anxious voice Norman instantly recognized as his mother's.

A clap of thunder erupted overhead like a burst of demonic laughter.

"He's in charge!" someone called. "Get him!"

"Hang him!" cried another voice.

"Hey, now, stop that kind of talk," shouted Sheriff Hooper. "We're civilized people here—we don't hang folks anymore."

Finally. One sane person.

"Then burn him!" yelled another voice.

Norman heard the voice of his mother over the crowd. "Can you all stop being a mob for one second?"

It was followed by his father's voice calling, "Son, step away from the zombies."

Norman saw his parents then, stepping out of the crowd, gesturing for him to come down to them.

"No!" he yelled at them.

"Enough dillydallying," bellowed Crystal, still wielding her shotgun. "We've got to get *them* before they get us!"

That seemed to be what the mob was waiting to hear. Were they blind? Could they really no longer distinguish children from zombies? The crowd began to surge forward, lifting their weapons. In a split second, Courtney dashed onto the steps, placing herself between the mob and her zombie-flanked brother. Mitch and Neil were immediately at her side, and making himself as small as possible behind Mitch was Alvin.

"Stop!" Courtney cried. "Guys, grab each other's hands."

Alvin bodychecked Neil to get next to Courtney. He regretted it when he realized her intention was to create a living fence between the mob and Norman. Well, if he died holding Courtney Babcock's hand, it would be worth it. The crowd stopped their push forward. Courtney had their attention.

"For Pete's sake, does it look like anybody is about to attack you?" she called. "That's my brother standing behind me with those zombies. And right now, we all need to listen to him. I know it might seem crazy—believe me, I'm with you on that—but maybe he does actually know what he's talking about."

"All night, we've been trying to help Norman save you all from the witch's curse," Neil chimed in.

"Yeah, and all you guys want to do is burn and murder stuff, burn and murder stuff. Just burning and murdering!" Mitch added.

"Shame on every single one of you!" shouted Alvin, momentarily forgetting his own glowing history of bullying the innocent and the meek. "How dare you all?"

"Those are the evil dead up there!" cried Sheriff Hooper, waving around a pair of handcuffs.

"No," Norman said. The crowd fell silent. "They're just people. Or they used to be. Stupid people who should have known better."

"So...they're not going to hurt us?" asked Crystal, half lowering her shotgun.

"No! The curse isn't about them hurting *you*. It's about you hurting *them*."

Norman could see that the anger in the mob was beginning to leave. Some of them were looking at one another a little sheepishly. They were becoming individuals again.

"They did something unforgivable," Norman said,

pointing at the zombies who were all standing perfectly still behind him. "And they were cursed for it. That's why they're zombies. But it has to stop now—it has to stop for good."

As if a silent signal had been given, the people began putting their weapons on the ground. Norman caught sight of his mother's face—she looked frightened and hopeful. His father looked grim.

A little girl Norman recognized from school tentatively stepped forward, climbing the steps, clutching something in her hands. It was an arm. Norman watched as she silently approached a one-armed zombie. She held out her hands and gave him his arm back.

Norman sighed with relief. Okay. Things were going to be all right now.

But the quiet was suddenly pierced by a deafening scream from the sky. Everyone looked up. The sky was bloodred, and the clouds were alive, swirling into a vast vortex that seemed to undulate and move with intelligence. As it swirled, a blast of wind hit the courthouse, which was still burning. Fueled by the wind, the building erupted in a fireball, tongues of white flames shooting out.

The crowd scattered in terror, and Norman and Neil ran down the steps and dove behind a parked car for cover.

"What's happening?" Neil asked. "Do you think you made her angrier?"

A blast of lightning shot out of the vortex into the town square, striking the statue of the witch and cracking it. Another blast of wind sent the statue teetering on its base, and it momentarily lifted in the air before crashing onto the Town Hall steps, shattering into countless chunks of rubble. The whirlwind raged down Main Street, blowing out the windows of the tacky tourist shops and ripping through the huge billboard in the plaza, leaving nothing but splinters of wood in its wake.

Norman stood up and struggled through the wind toward a group, townspeople and zombies alike, who had remained behind and were cowering in fear. His parents were among them.

"Norman!" his mother cried, pouncing on him with a crushing hug as Neil and the others reached them.

"Mom, I'm fine," Norman mumbled into his mother's neck, struggling to get free.

"So what do we do now?" Neil asked.

And suddenly everybody was looking at him. Everybody expected Norman to know exactly what to do. People were finally taking him seriously and listening to him. And he had no idea what to say.

"I'm . . . I really don't know," Norman said. Because, actually? He was exhausted. He had had just about enough.

"Oh yes, you do know, Norman Babcock," Courtney said sharply. "You've got to get to that witch's grave, like, *now*. Before she destroys the entire town."

"But—"

"You listen to me, buster," Courtney interrupted. "We didn't turn away when Daleridge High was slaughtering our volleyball team, right?"

"I, uh, actually thought we did," Norman said.

"Not the cheerleaders," Courtney shot back. "I've cheered the uncheerable, Norman, and I am *not* going to let you give up now!"

Norman stared at his sister, almost not believing what he was hearing. His sister, the very same girl who frequently described him as the reason for all pain, was cheering him on. Cheering *him*. Like, in front of people.

Norman turned to his father, who might or might not have been aware that the zombie judge was standing next to him, hanging on every word.

"Dad," he said, in his most businesslike voice, "can I borrow the car?"

Three hundred years ago, a mob of Pilgrims had buried her body in an unmarked grave, leaving the forest to cover the evidence of their terrible deed.

Chapter Fifteen

Moments later, Perry Babcock started the engine of his station wagon and pulled onto the street, his wife sitting nervously in the front passenger seat. He glanced in the rearview mirror, hoping this was all just a trauma-induced hallucination.

But no. There was still a zombie in his car.

The dead judge was sitting rigidly between Courtney and Norman, his eyes staring straight ahead. Very discreetly, Mrs. Babcock pulled a small perfume bottle from her purse and gave the car a few spritzes. Occasionally, the judge would open his mouth, and the others would hear only a guttural groaning. But Norman could understand him and was acting as translator.

"Norman!" Courtney snapped. "Your friend is on my side of the seat."

Norman sighed and nudged the judge's rotting arm.

"She wants you to move over," Norman told him.

An unintelligible sound came from the judge's mouth.

"I heard that!" cried Courtney. "Moooom! Tell the zombie to stop saying stuff about me!"

"Can you please stop using the *Z* word?" Norman snapped.

"So help me, I *will* stop this car right now if all three of you don't quit it this instant!" exploded Mr. Babcock.

There were a few moments of silence, then the judge emitted a low, sepulchral moan.

"He says, 'Take a left here,'" Norman translated.

Mr. Babcock sighed but followed the directions. "We've already *been* this way!" he complained. "We're going around in circles."

"Maybe we should pull over and ask somebody," suggested Mrs. Babcock.

"Oh, right! Maybe we should stop at a graveyard and dig up some bodies and get directions from them!"

"It's not a bad idea, dear," Mrs. Babcock said, flipping down the mirror in the car and checking her reflection.

Mr. Babcock shook his head.

"I wish I understood you," he said.

Norman's eyes widened. He thought *he* was the only family member Mr. Babcock didn't understand.

As the car rounded a corner, something loomed in front of them.

"Look out!" screamed Mrs. Babcock.

A truck, caught in the grips of the spectral wind, was tumbling down the street, flipping over and over as if it were a child's toy. Norman's father swerved to miss the massive vehicle, which came close to crushing them.

Mrs. Babcock turned in amazement to watch the truck continue to roll down the road like tumbleweed.

"Boy, the traffic tonight!" she remarked.

The judge turned to Norman and made another low, weird groan.

"Now what?" snapped Mr. Babcock. "Please don't tell me he needs to use the bathroom."

"Turn that way," Norman translated, pointing. "Down there!"

The car veered off the road and onto a narrow dirt lane leading into the woods. The sky shimmered eerily through a massive vortex of luminous spectral clouds being funneled into the tree line just ahead.

"Oh my," Mrs. Babcock said. "Do you think that's it?"

Norman didn't answer. He just looked out the window. *Hex marks the spot,* he thought. And when the headlights fell on a massive downed tree across the path and the dead judge issued a one-syllable gurgle, Norman knew they could drive no farther. He would have to go the rest of the way on foot.

"I've got to get out of the car," Norman said.

"Why?" asked Mr. Babcock.

"Because, Dad, I've got to get to her grave and talk to her," Norman said, opening the door. "It's the only way to put a stop to this." For once, his dad didn't argue.

Outside the car, Norman could hear the trees creaking and groaning under the onslaught of the witch's furious storm. The judge stood beside Norman and pointed to a place deeply overgrown with bushes and brambles. Norman took a deep breath and plunged in.

As he forced his way forward, branches and limbs seemed to be grabbing at him. He could hear the others shouting, but that only made Norman force his way harder through the undergrowth.

Each time Norman pulled free of one obstacle, another limb or branch would come crashing down in front of him.

She knows I'm coming, Norman thought. *She'll do anything to stop me.*

Just several feet from where he was standing, a

massive tree uprooted itself and came thundering down, slamming into the ground and spraying him with bits of bark and earth. A split second after the impact, he heard Courtney shrieking his name. But his eye was caught on something up ahead, something that did not belong in the woods. Through the trees, the strange glowing light they had seen in the sky rippled through the swaying trees and seemed to pulse with a life of its own.

"I'm okay!" Norman shouted at his family. "Go back and wait in the car—you'll all be safer there."

Norman thought he heard his father call something, but he could not make it out over the howling of the wind and the sound of hundreds of tree branches slapping against one another. Norman staggered forward, ignoring the pain of twigs snapping into his face and brambles tearing at his jeans. As he got closer to the light, the undergrowth seemed to thin out, and suddenly Norman was walking on barren earth. Straight ahead of him lay a clearing. And in the center of the clearing were the remains of a long-dead tree, its trunk and remaining limbs grotesquely twisted and bleached white as bone. Norman did not need the judge to tell him that the remains of Agatha Prenderghast were buried at the foot of the twisted white tree. Three hundred years ago, a mob of Pilgrims had buried her body in an unmarked grave, leaving the forest to cover the evidence of their terrible deed.

The pulsating white-yellow light seemed to be emanating from the tree itself, rippling over a mess of roots and rocks on the ground. In the center of the rocks, Norman's eye caught a movement. He could make out a small, human-shaped form. It was then that Norman realized that the spitting furnace of spectral light and the violent storm it was creating weren't coming from the tree or the sky. They were coming from the small figure crouched among the roots and stones.

Norman felt a fear seep through his bones—the kind of fear in people in zombie movies who were literally convulsing with terror. Norman had never been so frightened in his life. He took a deep breath and took several steps forward.

"Hello?" he called.

Bad idea, an inner voice automatically told him. He did not want to attract the wrong kind of attention, such as a meat cleaver in the back. Or decapitation. Or something else not good.

A voice erupted around him, seeming to come from

every direction at once—coming as much from the inside of Norman's head as the outside.

You are not welcome here. Leave this place.

The wind howled even harder, and the trees seemed to shake and bow with terror.

"I need to speak with you," Norman called.

Leave this place, Norman heard again. The sound of the voice seemed to rush right through him, leaving him shaking and out of breath.

"I won't leave until I've spoken with you," Norman said. With each step he took toward the tree, a voice inside him shouted *No! Turn and run!* as if his brain were in the audience and he were nothing more than a character in a movie. A very scary movie.

Who are you?

"My name is Norman Babcock. You don't actually know me, but I know you. I'm your great-great-great... well, we're related. We're kind of the same, you and I."

He advanced two more steps as he spoke, but he still could not make out any details of the figure crouched in the roots of the tree. Light streamed from behind it, and jagged tendrils of liquid fire snaked from its head.

You are not dead.

"Well, no," Norman said. He took a step.

You are a boy.

"That's right." Another small step. At least she was talking now.

You are not like me at all.

Norman thought carefully before speaking. This could go either way now. He could reach her in some way, human to human, or he could return her to the cataclysmic tantrum she had been having.

"I know what you're feeling," Norman said, taking another step. He could feel the storm coming off her now. The fiery light was not hot, but it seemed to be exploding with electricity. The air crackled and snapped.

No. No one knows that. No one knows anything about me.

"Your name is Agatha Prenderghast."

There was a ripple in the light for a moment, as if someone had dimmed a switch and then powered it up again. *Progress,* Norman thought.

"And you're tired. I'm tired, too. It's late, and it's been a really long night, and nobody seems to understand us. And we're just kids. We should be home, in bed, with a glass of warm milk and a nice story—"

A crack of lightning shot skyward, silencing Norman.

I will not sleep! You cannot make me sleep! I burned your book to dust so I will never have to hear your stupid stories. Now **LEAVE ME ALONE!**

The voice had risen to a high-pitched shriek—the sound of a spoiled toddler who was not getting what she wanted and was unleashing the fury of a tantrum. A branch crashed down to Norman's right, and a clump of mud whizzed by his head.

"I won't leave. Not until you listen to me."

The wind seemed to die down for a moment. She was listening. But she was right—she had destroyed the book. What was he supposed to do now? Make up a new fairy tale to tell her? Something to replace the story from the book?

"So, okay—well, once upon a time there was a...a little girl," Norman said.

I'm tired of the same old story. Go away and leave me alone.

Something about her tone was beginning to change. Her voice was still eerie, bouncing off the trees and off the inside of Norman's skull, but she was also beginning to sound more childlike. *I think she's forgotten she ever was a child,* Norman thought. *I shouldn't treat her like a monster; I should treat her like what she is. A little girl.*

"Just listen," Norman said. "This isn't a fairy tale. It's a different kind of story. So...the little girl lived in a village, but she was different from all the other people there."

I'm not listening. **NOT LISTENING. LA LA LA LA LA LA LA LA.**

The sound of her chanting almost split Norman's skull, but he realized it was a very childlike thing to do. That meant he was making progress.

"The little girl would see and do things that no one else could understand. That made them scared of her."

I do **NOT** *like this story!*

"So she turned away from everyone and became sad and lonely. No one understood her. She had no one to turn to."

STOP IT!

Norman had advanced three more steps during the story. He could make out Agatha's features now—her face glowing and ghostly and still contorted with anger.

He could also see that she was not on the ground, but was rather floating several feet above it.

"But the more the girl turned away from people, the more they feared her. Their fear grew and grew, and one day they did something terrible."

Multiple arcs of blue-white energy cracked through the air, sizzling and sputtering like comets. When they hit the ground, each one exploded in a fury of white flame.

"They came and took the girl. They took her away."

Norman took a final step forward and dropped his voice.

"They killed her," he said quietly.

No. No. **NOOOOOO!**

"But she was more powerful than they imagined. And very angry. She put a curse on everyone who had harmed her. And then later, even though she was dead, something in her came back."

STOP!

"The part that came back forgot it was Agatha. That part that came back was anger, and revenge. And it wouldn't go away, not for the last three hundred years."

SHUT UP!

"And every year, the revenge part got stronger, and

the little-girl part got weaker. But she's still in there. You're still in there, Agatha."

I WILL MAKE YOU SUFFER!

Norman held his hands out to the floating, glowing specter.

"Why?" he asked softly.

Because you . . . because . . .

"Because they hurt you, and you wanted to hurt them back. And every year, when you wake up, you play this mean game. But you don't play fair!"

They hurt me!

Norman remembered Agatha's dirty, tearstained little face in the courthouse, and his heart ached. But this was not the time to give her sympathy. Agatha was out of control. Her galactic temper tantrum was going to consume the entire town. Kind words were not going to snap her out of her rage.

"So you hurt them back."

I wanted everyone to see how rotten they were.

"Which makes you exactly like them."

I am not! **I AM NOT LIKE THEM!**

"You are. You're a bully."

I AM NOT A BULLY!

This was the moment. He had to reach her now—he had to get through to her. Norman held his head high and walked right into the cloud of crackling, fiery light.

"They did something awful to you. But that doesn't give you the right to do the same thing."

Now that he was standing inside the light, Norman could see her clearly. Her long dark hair snaked and writhed around her head. Her body rippled with liquid fire, and plumes of electric light exploded off her. But even so, Norman could see now what was underneath. For all her tempestuous fury, Agatha was still just a little girl.

"All that's left of you is mean and horrible!" Norman shouted.

That isn't true!

Norman stepped onto a tree root so he could get close enough to Agatha to touch her. The heat and fire seared his skin, but he reached his hands closer to her in spite of the burning pain.

"Then prove it! Stop this! It's wrong, and you know it. Agatha, you've spent so long remembering what the bad people did to you, you've forgotten there are good people in the world, too. There must be someone who loved you and cared about you. Don't you remember?"

Keep away from me—just keep away!

Norman was reaching up toward Agatha, but he wasn't quite close enough to touch her. He closed his eyes and took a deep breath.

"Remember!" he shouted.

And then he jumped up—into the light.

"—there's really no scientific way to quantify what infectious diseases a zombie might be capable of—"

Chapter Sixteen

Norman saw a brilliant flash of white light, visible even through his tightly closed eyes. Then nothing.

When he opened his eyes, the world had completely changed.

Gone were the gnarled old trees with their rotting limbs. Gone was the barren earth of the clearing. Gone were the wind, the lightning, the tempest. Gone was the night sky.

Norman was sitting on the ground with the sun streaming down. There was something warm against his hand. Carefully, he opened his eyes. The forest floor was carpeted with grass and wildflowers, and overhead was a canopy of golden-green leaves, sunlight pouring through them. Agatha's tree was young and strong, its bark thick and healthy, its branches heavy with leaves and tiny scented blossoms.

The air smelled of young wood and fresh earth

and flowers. His hand, still outstretched, touched just one finger on the hand of the girl. Norman couldn't take his eyes off the small white hand touching his own. Then, slowly, he looked up at Agatha's face. Her bright blue eyes were staring into his, her long dark hair falling softly around her face.

"I'm Aggie. They called me Aggie," she said.

Norman nodded, speechless. She was so small. She was so real.

A brightly colored butterfly elegantly glided past them. Aggie turned to look at it, her eyes wide.

"I...I remember..." Aggie began in a faltering voice. "I remember my mommy brought me here once. We sat under this tree. She told me stories. The kind with happy endings."

Norman nodded and smiled. He didn't want to say anything yet. He wanted to make sure this new, quiet Aggie was staying, and the wild, vengeful Agatha was gone for good.

Aggie's brow furrowed as she struggled to remember.

"But then...but then those horrible men came. They took me away! They took me away, and I never saw her again!"

A flash of anger illuminated Aggie's eyes. When the

butterfly fluttered past again, Aggie's scowl deepened. There was a tiny puff, and the butterfly was gone, and a handful of blackened dust hung in the air in its place for a moment before falling to the ground.

The anger in Aggie's face disappeared, replaced by confusion, then sadness as she realized that her anger had just destroyed an innocent, beautiful thing.

"Aggie, sometimes when people get really scared, they say and do terrible things. We all do it sometimes. I think those men got you so scared that you forgot who you really were. They called you a witch. But I don't think you're a witch, Aggie. Not really."

Aggie stared at Norman, her eyes shiny with tears.

"You don't?" she whispered.

Norman shook his head.

"I think you're just a little kid with a really special gift. And you only wanted people to understand you." Norman smiled sadly at Aggie. "I know how that feels. I can talk to dead people, too, Aggie, just like you could. And people are mean to me because that scares them. Even my own dad is scared of me sometimes, and that hurts. It hurts when people are mean to me just because of who I am."

As he talked, Aggie had slipped her hand into his. He gave her hand a squeeze.

"So we're not all that different, you and me," Norman told her.

Aggie nodded.

"But then what about the people who hurt you?" she asked. "Don't you ever want to pay them back— don't you ever want to make them suffer for what they do?"

Norman thought for a few moments.

"Well, yeah, I think about it. But what good would it do? It would just make things worse. They would just hit back harder. And it does get better. Don't think just because there are bad people out there that there aren't any good ones. Don't think you have to go through everything alone. I thought the same thing. For a while."

Norman thought of Neil Downe. He thought of Courtney, and Mitch and Salma. He even thought of Alvin. In their own ways, each one of them had been his friend today.

"There's always someone out there for you. Somewhere. You just have to let them help you."

Aggie frowned and looked away.

"My mommy helped me. I want her back."

Norman looked down.

"I'm sorry, Aggie. She's gone. She died a long time ago. But I'm here. And I want to help you."

A fat tear rolled down Aggie's cheek, and she bit her lower lip.

"That story you were telling me," she said. "How does it end?"

"I think that's up to you," he told her quietly.

Aggie blinked through her tears and looked down at the grass beneath her feet.

"Is this where they buried me?" she asked.

Norman nodded.

"This was a beautiful place," he said. "I think it's a pretty good place to go to sleep. And if you did that, I think you could be with your mom again."

Aggie took a deep, shuddering breath, then her legs gave out, and she sat down hard on the grass, sobbing. Norman knelt down next to her, close enough so that she'd know, even with her eyes closed, that he was right there. She curled up on one side in the grass, her ragged sobs slowly giving way to calmer, deeper breathing. In the sun-dappled light, her face became serene, her long hair fanning out around her like a pillow.

Before Norman's eyes, the air took on a strange, out-of-focus quality. All the things around him began to dissolve, and in their place were golden bubbles of light. The glowing orbs swirled together in a spiral, dancing around like a whirlwind of pure sunlight. They spun upward in a wide column, reaching all the way up to the clouds he could glimpse overhead. Aggie's form dissolved into ribbons of glowing white light, and the world turned white around Norman. Far in the distance, there was a faint flash of lightning and a muffled rumble of thunder, the sounds of a powerful storm that had played itself out and was moving on. Norman closed his eyes and sent a silent farewell to Aggie.

She would be safe now. She had gone to sleep.

She had gone home.

• ◆ •

When Norman opened his eyes, it was night again. The clearing was once again burned and barren. The blanket of grass was gone, and Norman was sitting on the pointy, upturned root of the old tree, which was dead and bone white once again. Norman looked up at the sky where Aggie had gone with a sad smile.

"Sleep tight," he whispered.

Then he got up, and without looking back, he headed to the path and began walking to the car.

When he heard a strange hip-hop beat coming from his own pocket, Norman almost jumped out of his skin. Then he remembered he still had Courtney's phone.

"Hello?"

"Norman, it's me," Salma said. "I've been trying to get you forever—why weren't you answering the phone?"

"Sorry," Norman said. "I didn't hear it. I've been a little busy."

"Well, you need to know what's going on in the town square," Salma said. "You're not going to believe this."

Norman stopped walking, his heart sinking. He had truly thought the nightmare was over. Aggie had remembered who she was and had gone to sleep forever. Wasn't that supposed to stop the rest of it?

"Just tell me," Norman said wearily.

"Well, the zombies have all been standing in the center of the square since you left with your parents. All of them, except for that one who got in your car, which, by the way, concerns me from a strictly medical perspective because there's really no scientific way to quantify what infectious diseases a zombie might be capable of—"

"Salma, just tell me what they're doing!" Norman cried.

"I am," Salma said impatiently. "They've all been standing there staring at the sky. Just staring at it. They're ignoring all the townspeople. Sheriff Hooper shouted a few times, but they just ignored her, too. The whole town is standing there staring at them, and they don't seem to care. And now that the sky is starting to clear, something is happening to them!"

"What? What's happening?"

"I'd have to describe it as a form of transubstantiation, though I know the term can be controversial, and from a purely subjective point of view some might prefer to leave it at consubstantiation, but essentially... they're changing."

"Changing how?" Norman asked. He realized suddenly that the night air was chilly, and he was starting to feel very cold. He started walking again, the phone pressed to his ear.

"They're helping each other, taking each other's arms. Not taking them off, I mean. Holding each other upright. And their physical features are beginning to stabilize. I'd say they're undergoing some form of retroincarnation."

"Some form of what?" Norman could see headlights in the distance, and he began to walk faster.

"They're returning to the way they looked in their bodies, when they were alive. But they...oh!"

"What?" Norman asked.

"Oh, wow!"

"Salma, what's happening?" Norman shouted.

"Their bodies are just dissolving now—just fading out, and they have become these...ghosts. I can see through them. They're floating just above the square and looking around. One of them is looking right at me!"

"Do they look angry?" Norman asked.

"No," Salma reassured him. "Not at all. They actually look really...sad."

The headlights were much closer now, and Norman could hear the sound of the engine running.

"Wait, Salma, you said you can see them? The— the ghosts? Can *everyone* see them?" he asked.

"Well, yeah. The whole town is pretty much just standing there staring. Oh, now they're changing again," Salma continued. "They're getting smaller. They're floating—they're just like little specks of light. The breeze is carrying them off. Oh, Norman. They're gone!"

Norman gave a great sigh of relief.

"Listen, Salma, I have to go," he said. "But it's okay now. You can leave the police station. The zombies aren't coming back."

"Are you sure?" Salma asked.

"I'm positive," Norman told her. "And Salma? Thanks. Thanks for helping me."

"Isn't that what friends are for?" she asked.

Norman smiled. "It is, yeah," he said. "See you soon."

He snapped the phone shut and walked as fast as he could, stepping on a brittle twig, which made a loud snapping sound.

"Norman, is that you?" he heard his mother call.

"Yeah, it's me," he answered, pushing away the final tangle of branches and brambles that lay between him and the car. "I'm okay," he added, emerging into the beam of the headlights.

Mrs. Babcock shrieked when she caught sight of Norman. She rushed to him and almost snapped every bone in his body, she hugged him so hard.

"My brave little man!" she cried. "I thought I was going to lose you!"

Norman struggled to get free.

"Mom, you're embarrassing me," he complained. I mean, it was one thing for Courtney to see this—she was family. But the dead judge was there, too, and being fawned over by his mom in front of a zombie made Norman feel, well, mortified.

"That's my job," Mrs. Babcock said cheerfully. But she let Norman go.

He took a step back. They were all looking at him—his mother with her so-happy-I'm-gonna-cry face, Courtney with an unexpected smile, and his father with a confused expression, like he was seeing Norman for the first time.

"Good job, Norman," Courtney said. Norman waited for her to add something sarcastic, but she didn't.

"Thanks," he said.

Mr. Babcock walked over to Norman and took a deep breath.

"Norman..." he began.

Norman braced himself for what he knew was coming.

"I...well done, son. Whatever it was that needed doing out there, you obviously did it."

Norman stared at his father, not quite believing

what he'd just heard. Had his father just said something nice about Norman's supernatural ability?

"So, uh, do you think we could get out of here now?" Mr. Babcock added, looking around nervously.

Norman grinned.

"I think so. Let me ask," he said. "Judge? What do you say?"

Judge Hopkins took a few unsteady steps forward. His jaw dropped open, and he made a low, rasping mumble. He was staring at Norman. He put what was left of his hands out and nodded, adding a whimpering little syllable.

"You're welcome," Norman replied.

The moment the words were out of Norman's mouth, the judge began to crumble. His extended hands and arms went first, turning to something like a sculpture made of dirt, then dissolving into streams of an ashlike substance that showered to the ground. After his arms and legs were gone, the rest of the judge sort of collapsed in on itself in a rain of dust. His head went last—it hung for a moment in midair, eyes mournfully pointed at Norman, then it, too, turned brown and grainy, and dropped to the ground with a small explosion of dirt. In his place stood a perfectly formed figure—the judge restored to his once-imposing form, save for the fact that he was completely transparent.

"Whoa," Courtney said.

Norman snuck a look at his father. Mr. Babcock had placed himself mostly behind Mrs. Babcock. He stared at what was left of the judge with his mouth hanging wide open.

The misty image of the man the judge had once been hung there for a moment, his sorrowful gaze still trained on Norman.

Before the thought was even completed in Norman's head, the judge literally flew into bits—his image replaced by thousands of glowing embers, as if he were nothing more than a campfire releasing burning ash into the sky.

Norman and his family stood and watched as the tiny orbs of light sailed away in every direction until they were gone.

Norman turned to his father, who was still standing with his mouth hanging wide open.

"So in answer to your question, Dad," Norman said, "definitely yes. We can get out of here now."

Norman waited a polite amount of time
before wiggling free.

Chapter Seventeen

"Really, Mom, Dad. I promise I'll be fine, and I'll be home in an hour."

Norman's parents were both swiveled around in the car, staring at Norman with twin expressions of worry.

"Seriously—everything's over! I just need to find my...my friends. They're here in the town square somewhere."

"Norman, it's been a very long day," Mrs. Babcock began. "I really think you ought to come home, where we can keep an eye on you."

"No, it's all right," Mr. Babcock said. "He'll be fine, Sandra. I think we all realize now that Norman can take good care of himself. Not to mention the rest of us. But we'll wait right here in the car for you, son."

Norman smiled. "Thanks, Dad. I'll come right back."

He opened the car door and climbed out onto the

sidewalk. Before he could slam the door, Courtney climbed out after him.

"I was...I mean, do you mind?" she asked Norman, shifting her weight from one foot to the other. "If I, like...tag along with you?"

"That's fine," Norman said. "Courtney's coming with me," he called before slamming the car door. As he glanced back, Norman caught a glimpse of his mother anxiously watching him through the side-view mirror.

Courtney was fixing him with a look as she unwrapped a piece of gum.

"What?" Norman asked.

"Look," she said, popping the gum into her mouth. "I know sometimes it may seem like I hate you, but I really don't."

"Yeah, I know," he said, which wasn't completely true. Sometimes he had to wonder.

Courtney twisted her ponytail in circles.

"It's just that you...you..."

Norman waited for her to finish. He knew all this stuff—he was weird, he was creepy, he was unpopular. He'd heard it all before. But Courtney was trying to be nice, so he waited for her to finish.

"It's just that…why does she never try to talk to *me?*"

Norman frowned with confusion for a moment, then figured out what she was trying to say. *That's what upsets her?* he thought, amazed. *Because I can talk to dead people, she thinks Grandma likes me better?*

"You mean Grandma, don't you?"

Courtney nodded and tried to smile, though she had started to cry. Some of her eyeliner was migrating down her face along with the one tear that had spilled out. Norman figured he'd better talk fast to avert a major disaster.

"She asks about you sometimes," Norman said.

Courtney made a little hiccup sound that was a cross between a sob and an exclamation of surprise.

"Really? She does?"

"Absolutely!" Norman said.

"Well, what does she say about me?"

"Lots of things," Norman told her, although the ones that were immediately coming to mind weren't necessarily compliments. "Like, for example, she says you should stop dressing like a bimbo."

Courtney laughed, wiping her face with her sleeve and smearing a streak of wet eyeliner over one cheek.

"She said that?"

"Yeah," Norman said. It was actually one of the nicer things she'd said.

"That is really sweet," Courtney said, smiling at her brother. "Thanks for telling me."

"Anytime," Norman said.

And though he'd had enough surprises in one day to last a lifetime, Norman got another one when Courtney grabbed him and gave him a hug every bit as crushing as the ones his mother gave.

Norman waited a polite amount of time before wiggling free. Then he reached up and rubbed the smeared eyeliner off Courtney's face.

"Thanks," she said. "So let's go find your friends."

● ◆ ●

Norman guessed that Neil was still somewhere in the town square, which was filled with excited people. He and Courtney caught snippets of conversations as they walked by.

"I really didn't do anything—it was the others," the stiletto-boot woman was saying into her cell phone.

Sheriff Hooper appeared to be having a very serious conversation with Mrs. Henscher.

"Oh, that wasn't really me," Mrs. Henscher was saying, waving her hands around for emphasis. "You know how it is. You join a mob and you say things. I was merely inhabiting a role."

On a bench, Crystal the shotgun-toting bar owner was chatting up a beefy-looking guy.

"Like the cheerleader said, some of them were just kids up there. Not that I ever would have harmed a living soul. I'm a total peacemaker—everybody says so."

Courtney shot Norman a look.

"It's like they were all there screaming and making threats, but nobody thinks they were personally involved," Courtney said disdainfully.

"The more things change, the more they stay the same," Norman murmured.

"Huh?" his sister asked, snapping her gum.

"I just think that's the same thing that happened to Aggie Prenderghast three hundred years ago. A bunch of people came together against her, but none of them could see in the moment that they were doing anything wrong. They were just doing what everybody else was doing."

"Seventh grade all over again," Courtney declared.

Scary, but very, very true, Norman thought.

They were walking by a bunch of teenagers, and Norman heard the familiar, thick voice of Alvin coming from its midst.

"Fighting zombies is, like, second nature to me, man. And, yeah, me and Norman are in a lot of the same classes. We're pretty much inseparable. Best buds. Actually, we do a lot of psychic investigations together— we're not zombie-exclusive. You should check out our blog!"

Norman grinned and shook his head.

"What, you and Alvin are, like, BFFs now?" Courtney asked, sneaking a glance over her shoulder at a couple of football players standing in the crowd.

"It's news to me," Norman said. "But, hey, if Alvin wants to act like my friend now, I'll take it. Getting beat up in school gets really old, really fast."

Courtney's hand shot out, and she gripped Norman's arm with the clutch of death.

"There he is. He's coming this way!" she hissed.

The "he" was apparently Mitch Downe, who was, in fact, striding toward them with the swagger and the confidence of a fireman.

"Do I look okay?" Courtney whispered, giving Norman a pleading look.

"Oh yeah," Norman said. "Uh, you look fine? I guess?"

Courtney gave Norman a blinding smile, then turned and pretended to look like Mitch Downe was the last person on the face of the planet she'd expected to see here, in little old Blithe Hollow.

"Oh, hey, Mitch! Like, what a surprise! How have you been?"

"Better since the zombies melted, I guess," he said. "I'm just heading out to meet someone."

"So, yeah," Courtney said as if they were in the middle of a long and cozy conversation. "I was thinking maybe we could catch a movie sometime? Something, like, not scary?"

Mitch was scanning the crowd for someone, but he turned to Courtney for a moment.

"Oh sure, that sounds great, Kathy. I bet you'll get along great with my boyfriend, actually. He doesn't do scary movies, either. A nice chick flick, maybe. See ya!"

Mitch sped off toward the crowd, waving enthusiastically at someone.

"You have got to be kidding me," Courtney

muttered. "He doesn't remember my name? I should have seen that coming—he was too perfect."

Norman gave Courtney a sympathetic nudge on the arm and, at the same time, noticed Neil surveying the wreckage of the witch statue.

"Oh good, there he is!" Norman said.

"Wow," Courtney remarked. "Didn't he used to irritate you? And now you sound totally psyched to see him."

"He used to. And I am," Norman said. "I'll see you back at the car in a sec."

"Sure," Courtney said, heading in the direction of the football players. "Catch ya later."

Norman groaned. Alvin's meaty influence was spreading.

"Hey, Norman!"

Norman smiled and waved at Neil, hurrying over to him. When Neil grabbed him and gave him a brisk man-hug, Norman didn't mind one bit.

"Boy, am I glad to see you!" Neil said.

"Likewise," Norman agreed.

"You did it!" Neil exclaimed, smacking Norman on the arm. "You stopped the witch's curse and made the zombies go away and saved pretty much everything!"

Norman looked at his feet.

"I guess," he said. "Listen, I wanted to say thanks. For helping me today and everything. But also for standing up for me all the time. Trying to be my friend when I didn't think I needed friends."

"Yeah, I did tell you we'd have more fun being alone together," Neil said. "Salma and I always do. We should all three hang out alone together."

"Definitely," Norman said. "Maybe even starting tomorrow. But I kind of told my parents I'd go home with them."

"I need to go, too. So you think everything is back to normal now?"

Norman took a look around the town square. There were stores with windows smashed in, billboards ripped to shreds, trees uprooted, and a plume of smoke still rising from the Town Hall.

"I think we're going to need a new 'normal,'" Norman said, giving Neil a wave good-bye.

Yeah. A new normal. Whatever that meant.

"What do they think we are, stupid?
Zombies don't look one thing like that!"

Chapter Eighteen

Norman listened to the newscaster with amusement.

TOURIST TOWN HIT BY MYSTERY TORNADO, read the text superimposed over images of the wreckage on Main Street.

"Anything is less scary than the truth," Norman muttered.

"Oh, that's just a bunch of baloney!" came Mr. Babcock's voice.

Here it comes, Norman thought, turning to face his father. But Mr. Babcock was pointing at the television.

"There was no tornado," Mr. Babcock said. "What a load of hooey! Why can't they just say what really happened? A three-hundred-year-old curse got slapped on a bunch of Pilgrims, and zombies roamed the town, and last night, the whole thing got out of control until Norman Babcock fixed it. What's so complicated about that?"

His dad coughed. And then he looked at Norman. "Right, son?"

This new version of Dad is going to take some getting used to, Norman thought.

But he liked it. Score one for the "new normal."

"I thought Saturday was the night they show those horror movies you like so much," Mr. Babcock grumbled.

"Oh, it is," Norman replied. "But Mom said maybe we should spend a little family time together tonight. You, me, Mom, and Courtney."

"What am I, chopped liver?" came a feisty voice from the couch.

"And Grandma," Norman added hastily, catching his grandmother's eye and mouthing *sorry.*

"Well," Mr. Babcock began slowly, "I guess I can hang out and watch your movie. I can't say the horror stuff is right up my alley or anything. But if you like it...I suppose I ought to try to get used to this paranormal stuff and all. I can't promise you I'm ever going to get all this ghost-talking stuff you do. But I...I am gonna try."

Norman felt a lump rise in his throat. On the couch next to his father, Grandma Babcock winked.

"Thanks," Norman murmured.

"Anyway, where's Sandra with that popcorn?" Mr. Babcock asked, looking around. On cue, Norman's mother came into the room with a huge bowl overflowing with popcorn.

"Dad's going to watch the movie with us," Norman said.

Mrs. Babcock exclaimed with delight. "Why, Perry, that's wonderful! What's playing tonight, Norman?"

Norman stared at his mother for a moment. He still could not quite believe everyone was going to watch his movie with him.

"Cat got your tongue?" asked Grandma Babcock. "Aren't you happy the family is taking an interest in your...hobby?"

"I don't know," Norman said. "I think so."

"What?" asked Mr. and Mrs. Babcock simultaneously.

"No, sorry, I mean the movie's called *Death Dirge in Detroit.*"

"Oh, that sounds absolutely darling," Mrs. Babcock said, sitting down on the couch and very nearly ending up in Grandma Babcock's lap.

"No, I can't tonight," came Courtney's voice, followed shortly by Courtney herself as she came into the living room. Her ear was pressed to her phone, and she was dressed head to toe in pink, fluffy letters across her T-shirt spelling out I'M OUT OF YOUR LEAGUE. "No, yeah, not tonight. Got family plans—we're watching a movie with my brother, Norman—the one who, like, had a major convo with that witch and totes sent an army of zombies packing?"

"Here you go, Norman," said Mr. Babcock, tossing him the remote. He made as if to sit down in the middle of the couch, his not-inconsiderably-sized butt threatening to squash Grandma Babcock altogether.

"Uh, Dad?" Norman said, making a move-to-your-left gesture.

Mr. Babcock froze for a moment, looking very hard at the space in the center of the couch.

"Um, sorry about that, Mom," he said.

"No problem, but you could stand to miss a few meals," Grandma Babcock told him.

Mr. Babcock shot a questioning look at Norman, pointing at a small area at the very edge of the couch.

"She says no problem," Norman said. "And you'll be fine right there."

"Anyway, like I said, I have to go," Courtney was saying. She caught Norman's eye, pointed to the phone, then made a yak-yak-yak motion with her hand while rolling her eyes. "No, yeah, I'll ask him. I will. Okay, then—catch ya later."

Courtney snapped the phone shut, grabbed a pillow, and flopped down on the far end of the couch, leaving the middle free for Grandma.

"That was Stan Lobotini," Courtney said. "As in first-string quarterback! It's, like, the third time he called today. I might go out with him; I haven't decided yet."

"Why does she always go for the jock knuckle-draggers?" Grandma Babcock asked. "What's wrong with a nice honor roll student for a change? It's amazing how some people just can't see past a football jersey."

"Grandma Babcock says that's amazing," Norman told his sister.

Courtney swiveled around to look at the space on the couch between her parents.

"Thanks, Grandma!" she exclaimed.

"And that lip gloss is a little over the top," Grandma Babcock added. "She looks like a hussy."

"Anyway, I guess it's about time for the movie to start," Norman said quickly.

"Cool," Courtney said. "Oh, I'm supposed to ask you, Norman—Stan has to do a report on Julius Caesar for his ancient-history class, and he was wondering if you could get him an interview."

"Um, I'm not sure it works that way, but I can give it a shot," Norman said.

"Awesome," Courtney said, flopping onto her stomach and propping up her chin with her hands.

Norman changed the television to channel 486, which had recently shortened its name to HoGoNe from the Horror and Gore Network. The movie was just beginning—the titles flashing on-screen in bloodred dripping letters and the music a frenzy of organ notes and electric guitar riffs.

Mrs. Babcock reached up and switched off the lamp.

"What did she do that for?" asked Grandma Babcock.

"What did you do that for?" asked Mr. Babcock.

"Atmosphere," Mrs. Babcock said. "And it makes the movie scarier."

"No, it doesn't," said Grandma Babcock.

"No, it doesn't," said Mr. Babcock.

"Shhhh," hissed Courtney.

"When did Courtney get so bossy?" asked Grandma Babcock.

"Beats me," Mr. Babcock muttered.

Norman turned around and stared at his father with surprise. For a minute, it almost seemed like he had heard Grandma Babcock himself.

"What did you say, dear?" asked Mrs. Babcock.

"Nothing," Mr. Babcock said, looking around and blinking with confusion. Norman stared at him for another moment, then turned back toward the television, a tiny smile on his face.

On the screen, a grave digger with enormous, bulging eyes stood wielding a shovel over a grave marked with an ancient, crumbling headstone. He raised his shovel as if to thrust it deep into the earth. The music changed to one high, quavering note on the organ, and the grave digger looked around nervously.

"What's happening?" asked Mr. Babcock and Grandma Babcock simultaneously.

"Just watch," Norman told them.

A thing was coming out of the shadows directly behind the grave digger. It had white skin with black circles around each eye, and green hair.

"What's that supposed to be?" Norman's father and Grandma asked at the same time.

"A zombie," Norman told them.

"Oh, give me a break," Mr. Babcock said. "What do they think we are, stupid? Zombies don't look one thing like that!"

Norman reached for the bowl of popcorn his mother was offering him, then turned back toward the television, its greenish-blue light falling on Norman's face, which was lit with a happy, comfortable grin.

The new normal had begun.

Acknowledgments

Grateful acknowledgment and thanks to the amazing Chris Butler, the geniuses at Laika Films, and the incomparable Erin Stein.

Witch Trials
On Trial

A Follow-Up Extra-Credit Report

By Salma Ramsay

A

TRYAL

OF

WITCHES,

AT

BLITHE HOLLOW

HELD AT

Bury St. Edmonds for the County
of *New England;* on the
Tenth day of *March,* 1664.

BEFORE

Sir Matthew Hale Kt.

THEN

*Lord Chief Baron of His Majesties
Court of EXCHEQUER.*

Taken by a Person then Attending the Court

Blithe Hollow,
Printed for *William Shrewsbery* at the
Bible in *Duck-Lane.* 1682.

An example of a town notice announcing
a trial from the 1600s.

In the 1600s, a series of events occurred in Massachusetts that we now refer to as the Salem witch trials. It began with a group of young girls behaving strangely and having odd fits in which they acted possessed. After being pressured by adults, the girls said they were the victims of a witch's spell and accused several local women of witchcraft. The accused women were thrown in jail, and the accusations grew more widespread. By the time the trials ended in 1693, more than two hundred people had been tried for witchcraft, and twenty of them had been put to death. Eventually, it became accepted that the witch hunts had been based on lies and hysteria. The government even made an official apology. But the hysteria surrounding witches was like a bad flu—it spread quickly from town to town. And three hundred years ago, Blithe Hollow caught the bug.

A girl named Agatha Prenderghast lived in Blithe Hollow with her mother. If she were alive today, she would have attended the same school I do now. Agatha had a unique ability. She was able to speak to the dead. In this day and age, that probably would have made her an instant celebrity. She'd have written a book and gotten her own TV show. But three hundred years ago, people were scared of what Agatha could do. And when word of the Salem witch trials reached Blithe Hollow, that fear turned deadly. Agatha was accused of witchcraft, found guilty, and executed.

Today, Agatha Prenderghast and the witch trials have become a kind of motto for Blithe Hollow. We have witch-themed stores and gimmicks everywhere. But is that really something to be proud of? Are we remembering Agatha for the wrong reasons? Are we celebrating something we ought to be ashamed of?

We no longer accuse one another of witchcraft, not even here at Blithe Hollow Middle School. But we do still gang up on each other. We still feel safest when the attention is on someone else—when we are not the person being made fun of or called a name. Sometimes we may even join in, laughing at the person who has been singled out—because we are

An etching from the trial of the Blithe Hollow Witch.

safer that way, when we are part of the crowd. Or are we?

We've come a long way since our ancestors joined their friends and neighbors in accusing one another of witchcraft in what, as far as I'm concerned, was just plain bullying. I would like to suggest that we are not out of the woods yet. Just because we don't put people on trial and condemn them to death doesn't mean we have stopped hiding in the mob mentality. So I propose a change be made in Blithe Hollow. I ask that we remember Agatha Prenderghast not because she was a witch but because she *wasn't* one. I think we should remember her so we realize that we're all still capable of making mistakes and of treating people badly. I think she should be remembered as a citizen of Blithe Hollow, someone's child, someone's neighbor, someone's friend. Just like you and me.

OLD GRAVE YARD REMEMBERED -This forgotten graveyard serves as home to Blithe Hollow's most revered founders who saved the town from the dreaded witch's curse.

An example of how history was rewritten—
a photo and caption from old Town Hall records.